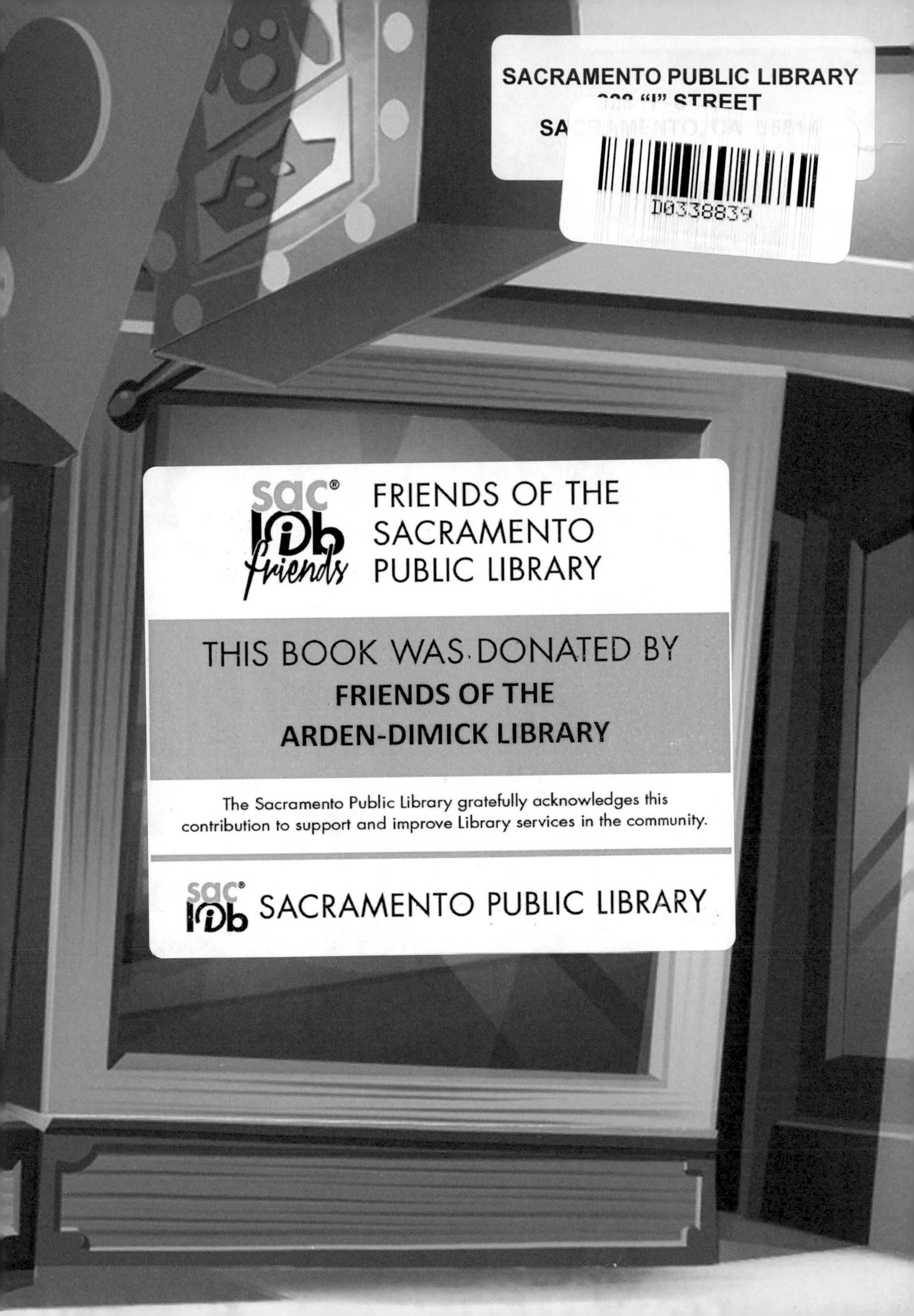

Geronimo Stilton™ Reporter

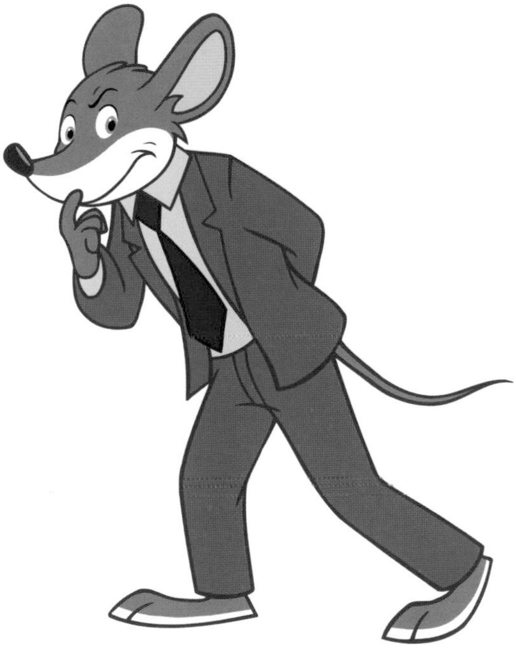

PAPERCUTZ™

Geronimo Stilton

GRAPHIC NOVELS AVAILABLE FROM PAPERCUTZ

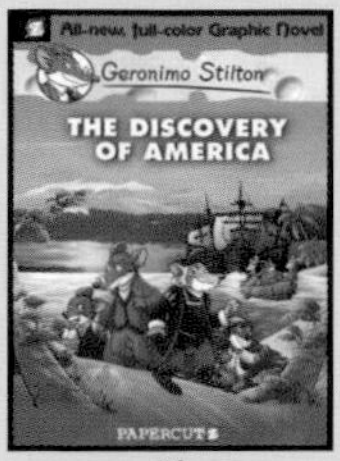
All-new, full-color Graphic Novel
Geronimo Stilton
THE DISCOVERY OF AMERICA
PAPERCUTZ
#1
"The Discovery of America"

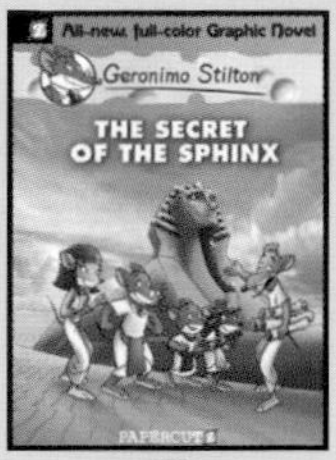
All-new, full-color Graphic Novel
Geronimo Stilton
THE SECRET OF THE SPHINX
PAPERCUTZ
#2
"The Secret of the Sphinx"

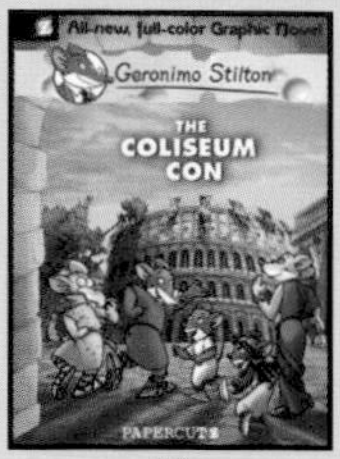
All-new, full-color Graphic Novel
Geronimo Stilton
THE COLISEUM CON
PAPERCUTZ
#3
"The Coliseum Con"

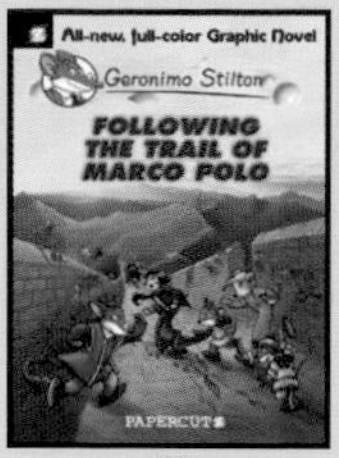
All-new, full-color Graphic Novel
Geronimo Stilton
FOLLOWING THE TRAIL OF MARCO POLO
PAPERCUTZ
#4
"Following the Trail of Marco Polo"

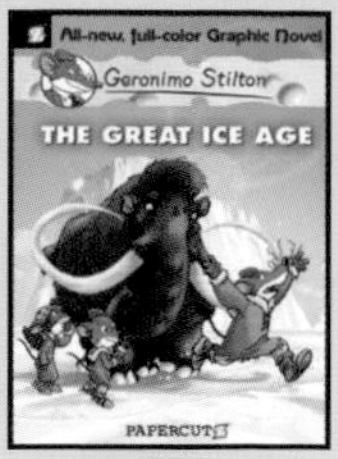
All-new, full-color Graphic Novel
Geronimo Stilton
THE GREAT ICE AGE
PAPERCUTZ
#5
"The Great Ice Age"

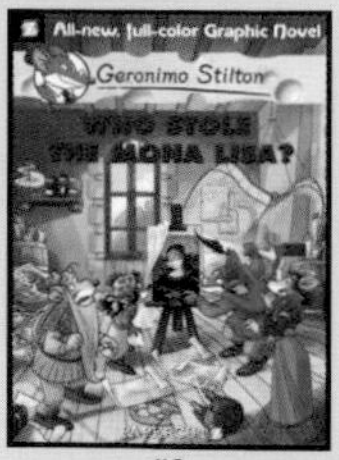
All-new, full-color Graphic Novel
Geronimo Stilton
WHO STOLE THE MONA LISA?
#6
"Who Stole The Mona Lisa?"

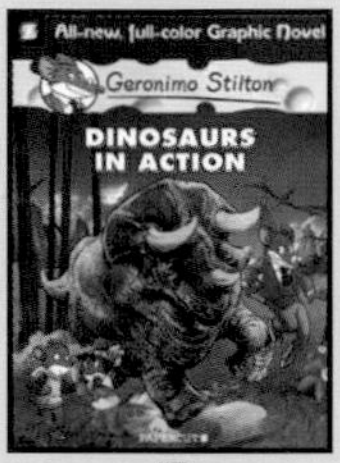
All-new, full-color Graphic Novel
Geronimo Stilton
DINOSAURS IN ACTION
#7
"Dinosaurs in Action"

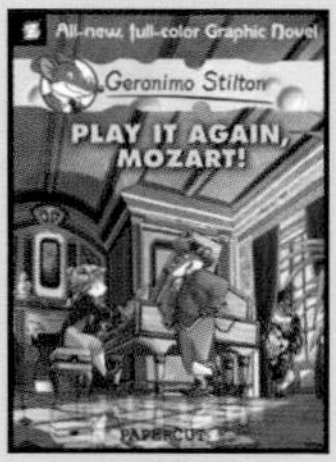
All-new, full-color Graphic Novel
Geronimo Stilton
PLAY IT AGAIN, MOZART!
#8
"Play It Again, Mozart!"

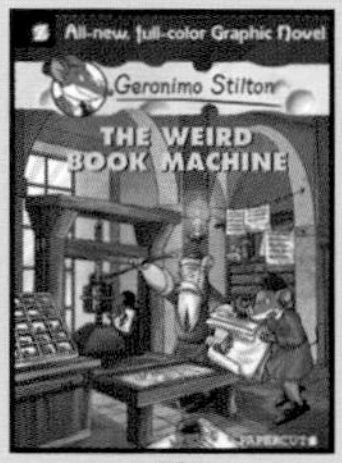
All-new, full-color Graphic Novel
Geronimo Stilton
THE WEIRD BOOK MACHINE
#9
"The Weird Book Machine"

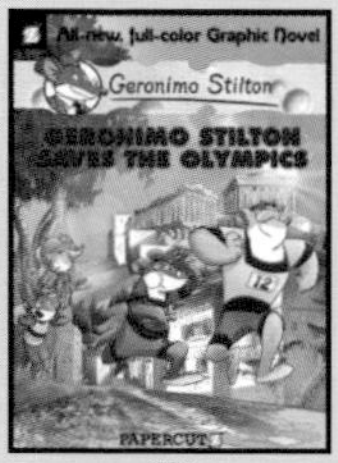
All-new, full-color Graphic Novel
Geronimo Stilton
GERONIMO STILTON SAVES THE OLYMPICS
#10
"Geronimo Stilton Saves the Olympics"

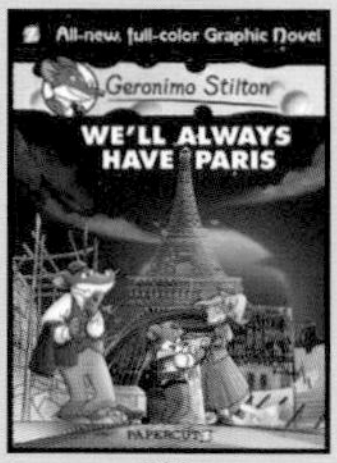
All-new, full-color Graphic Novel
Geronimo Stilton
WE'LL ALWAYS HAVE PARIS
#11
"We'll Always Have Paris"

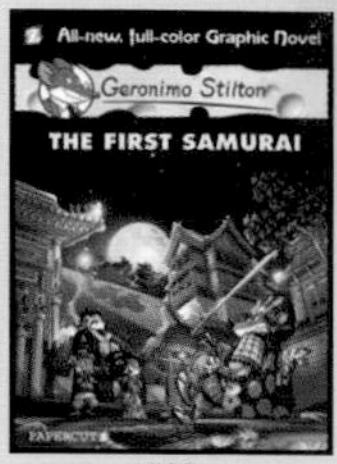
All-new, full-color Graphic Novel
Geronimo Stilton
THE FIRST SAMURAI
#12
"The First Samurai"

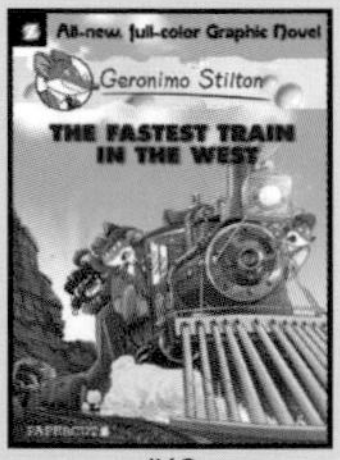
All-new, full-color Graphic Novel
Geronimo Stilton
THE FASTEST TRAIN IN THE WEST
PAPERCUTZ
#13
"The Fastest Train in the West"

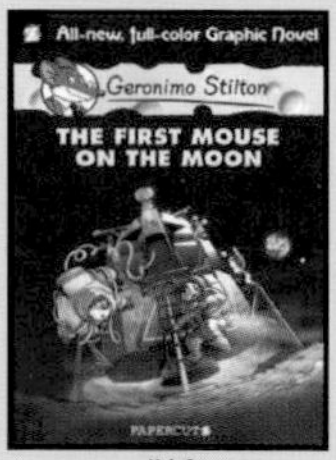
All-new, full-color Graphic Novel
Geronimo Stilton
THE FIRST MOUSE ON THE MOON
PAPERCUTZ
#14
"The First Mouse on the Moon"

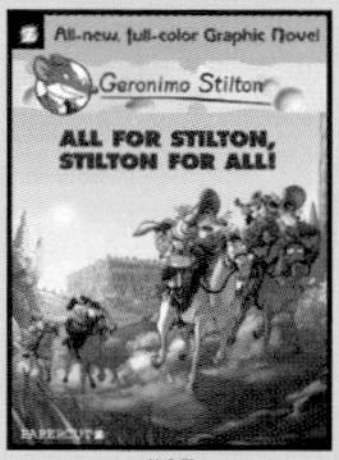
All-new, full-color Graphic Novel
Geronimo Stilton
ALL FOR STILTON, STILTON FOR ALL!
PAPERCUTZ
#15
"All for Stilton, Stilton for All!"

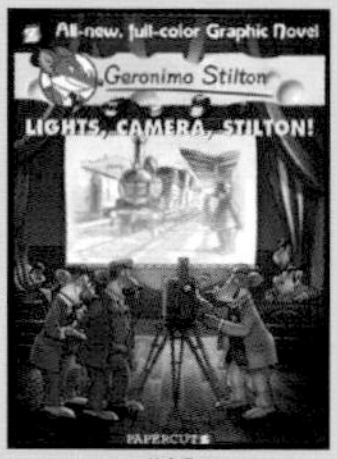
All-new, full-color Graphic Novel
Geronimo Stilton
LIGHTS, CAMERA, STILTON!
PAPERCUTZ
#16
"Lights, Camera, Stilton!"

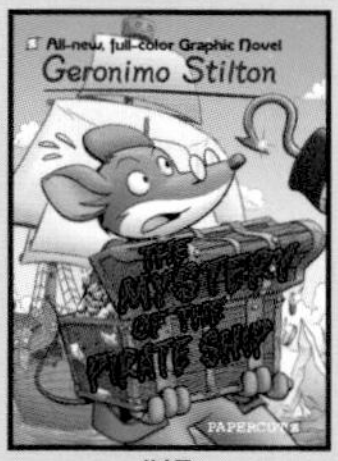
All-new, full-color Graphic Novel
Geronimo Stilton
THE MYSTERY OF THE PIRATE SHIP
#17
"The Mystery of the Pirate Ship"

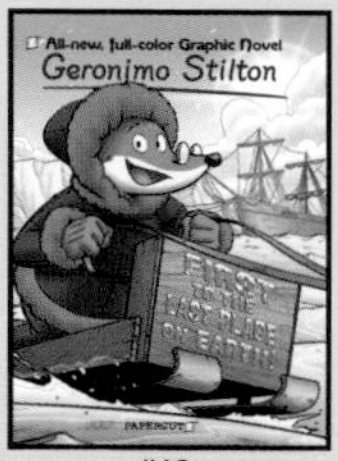
All-new, full-color Graphic Novel
Geronimo Stilton
#18
"First to the Last Place on Earth"

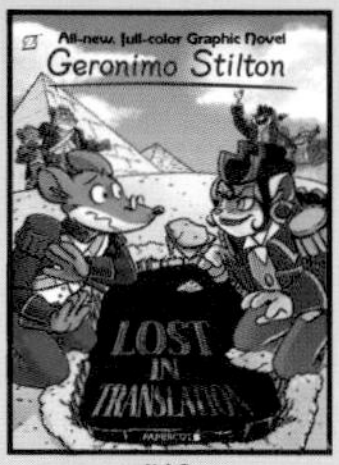
All-new, full-color Graphic Novel
Geronimo Stilton
LOST IN TRANSLATION
#19
"Lost in Translation"

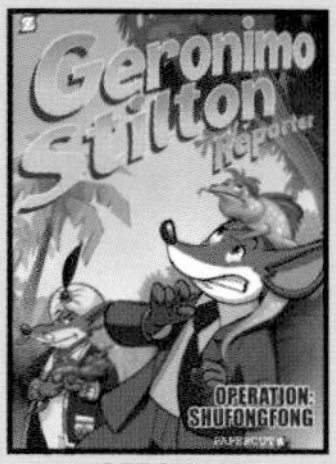
Geronimo Stilton Reporter
OPERATION: SHUFONGFONG
PAPERCUTZ
GERONIMO STILTON REPORTER #1
"Operation ShuFongfong"

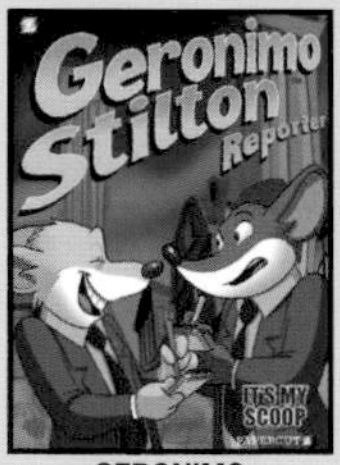
Geronimo Stilton Reporter
IT'S MY SCOOP
PAPERCUTZ
GERONIMO STILTON REPORTER #2
"It's My Scoop"

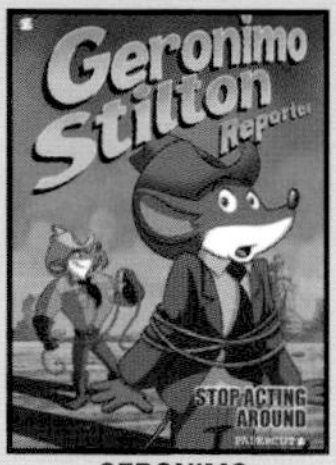
Geronimo Stilton Reporter
STOP ACTING AROUND
PAPERCUTZ
GERONIMO STILTON REPORTER #3
"Stop Acting Around"

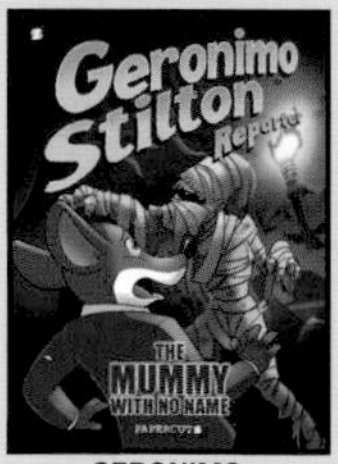
Geronimo Stilton Reporter
THE MUMMY WITH NO NAME
PAPERCUTZ
GERONIMO STILTON REPORTER #4
"The Mummy with No Name"

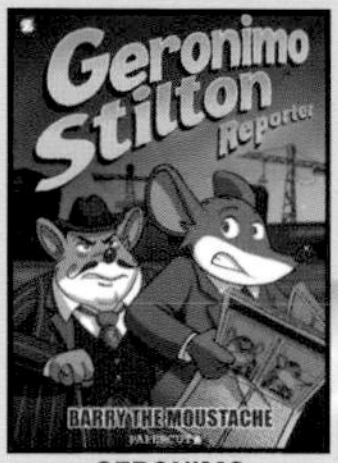
Geronimo Stilton Reporter
BARRY THE MOUSTACHE
PAPERCUTZ
GERONIMO STILTON REPORTER #5
"Barry the Moustache"

COMING SOON

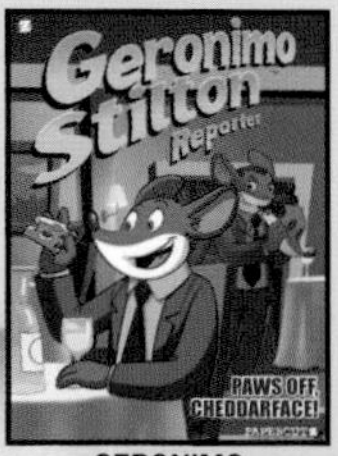
Geronimo Stilton Reporter
PAWS OFF, CHEDDARFACE!
PAPERCUTZ
GERONIMO STILTON REPORTER #6
"Paws Off, Cheddarface!"

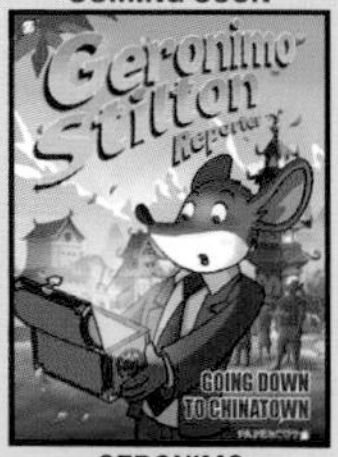
Geronimo Stilton Reporter
GOING DOWN TO CHINATOWN
GERONIMO STILTON REPORTER #7
"Going Down to Chinatown"

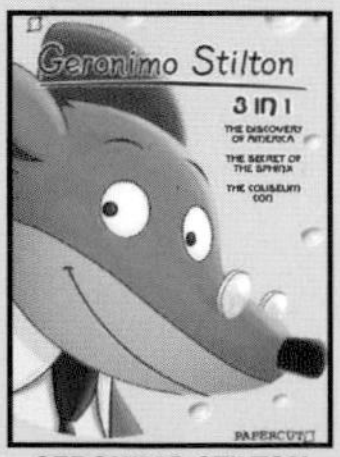
Geronimo Stilton
3 IN 1
THE DISCOVERY OF AMERICA
THE SECRET OF THE SPHINX
THE COLISEUM CON
PAPERCUTZ
GERONIMO STILTON 3 in 1 #1

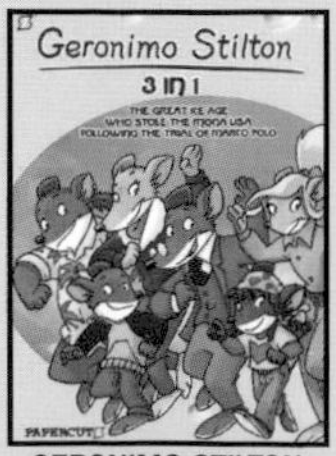
Geronimo Stilton
3 IN 1
THE GREAT ICE AGE
WHO STOLE THE MONA LISA
FOLLOWING THE TRAIL OF MARCO POLO
PAPERCUTZ
GERONIMO STILTON 3 in 1 #2

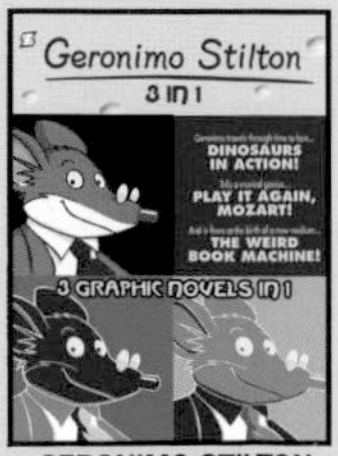
Geronimo Stilton
3 IN 1
DINOSAURS IN ACTION!
PLAY IT AGAIN, MOZART!
THE WEIRD BOOK MACHINE!
3 GRAPHIC NOVELS IN 1
GERONIMO STILTON 3 in 1 #3

...ALSO AVAILABLE WHEREVER E-BOOKS ARE SOLD!

See more at papercutz.com

Geronimo Stilton Reporter™

#6 PAWS OFF, CHEDDARFACE!
By Geronimo Stilton

PAPERCUTZ™

NEW YORK

PAWS OFF, CHEDDARFACE!
Geronimo Stilton names, characters and related indicia are copyright, trademark and exclusive license of Atlantyca S.p.A.
All right reserved.
The moral right of the author has been asserted.

Text by Geronimo Stilton
Cover by ALESSANDRO MUSCILLO (artist) and CHRISTIAN ALIPRANDI (colorist)
Editorial supervision by ALESSANDRA BERELLO (Atlantyca S.p.A.)
Editing by ANITA DENTI (Atlantyca S.p.A.)
Script by DARIO SICCHIO
Art by ALESSANDRO MUSCILLO
Color by CHRISTIAN ALIPRANDI
Original Lettering by MARIA LETIZIA MIRABELLA

Special thanks to CARMEN CASTILLO

TM & © Atlantyca S.p.A. Animated Series © 2010 Atlantyca S.p.A.– All Rights Reserved
International Rights © Atlantyca S.p.A., via Leopardi 8 - 20123 Milano - Italia - foreignrights@atlantyca.it - www.atlantyca.com
© 2020 for this Work in English language by Papercutz, 160 Broadway, Suite 700, East Wing, New York, NY 10038
www.papercutz.com

Based on an original idea by ELISABETTA DAMI.
Based on episode 6 of the Geronimo Stilton animated series "Giù le zampe, faccia di fontina!"
["Paws Off, Cheddarface"] written by CATHERINE CUENCA & PATRICK REGNARD storyboard by PIER DI GIÀ and PATRIZIA NASI
Preview based on episode 7 of the Geronimo Stilton animated series "Rotta verso la Cina" ["Going Down to Chinatown"]
written by LAURIE ISRAEL & RACHEL RUDERMAN storyboard by NICHOLAS MOSHINI

www.geronimostilton.com

Stilton is the name of a famous English cheese. It is a registered trademark of the Stilton Cheese Makers' Association.
For more information go to www.stiltoncheese.com

JAYJAY JACKSON — Production
WILSON RAMOS JR. — Lettering
JEFF WHITMAN — Managing Editor
JIM SALICRUP
Editor-in-Chief

ISBN: 978-1-5458-0546-6

Printed in China
October 2020

Papercutz books may be purchased for business or promotional use.
For information on bulk purchases please contact
Macmillan Corporate and Premium Sales
Department at (800) 221-7945x5442.

Distributed by Macmillan
First Printing

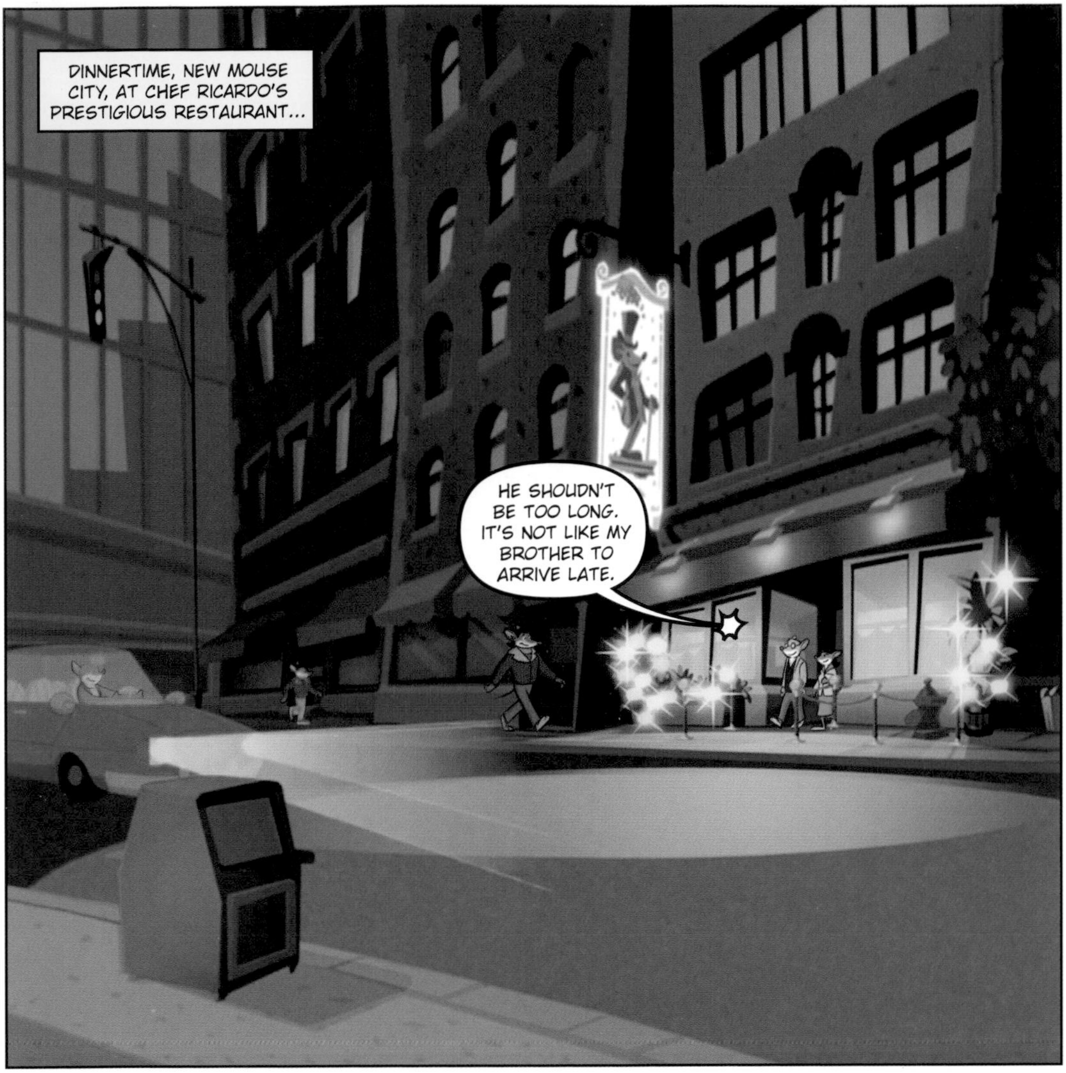
DINNERTIME, NEW MOUSE CITY, AT CHEF RICARDO'S PRESTIGIOUS RESTAURANT...
HE SHOUDN'T BE TOO LONG. IT'S NOT LIKE MY BROTHER TO ARRIVE LATE.

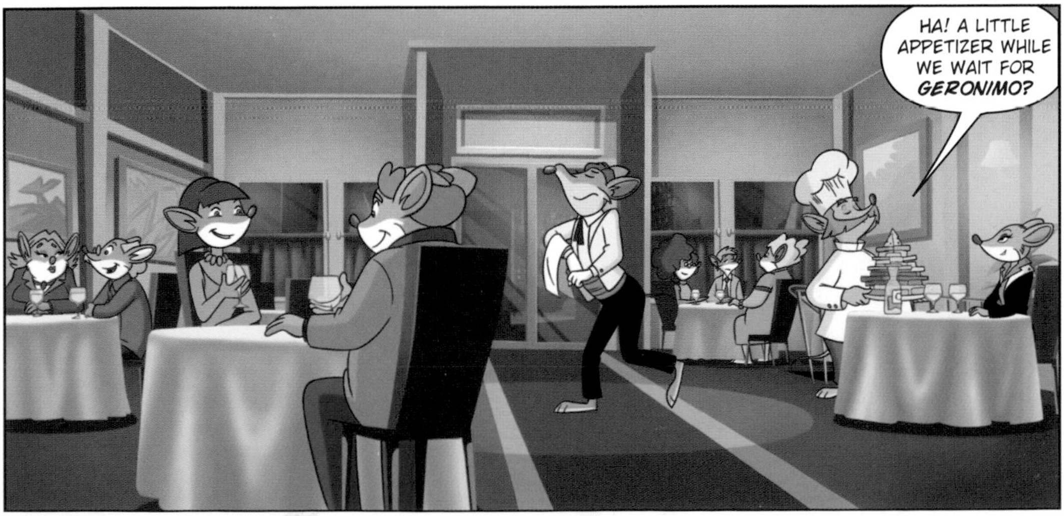
HA! A LITTLE APPETIZER WHILE WE WAIT FOR ***GERONIMO?***

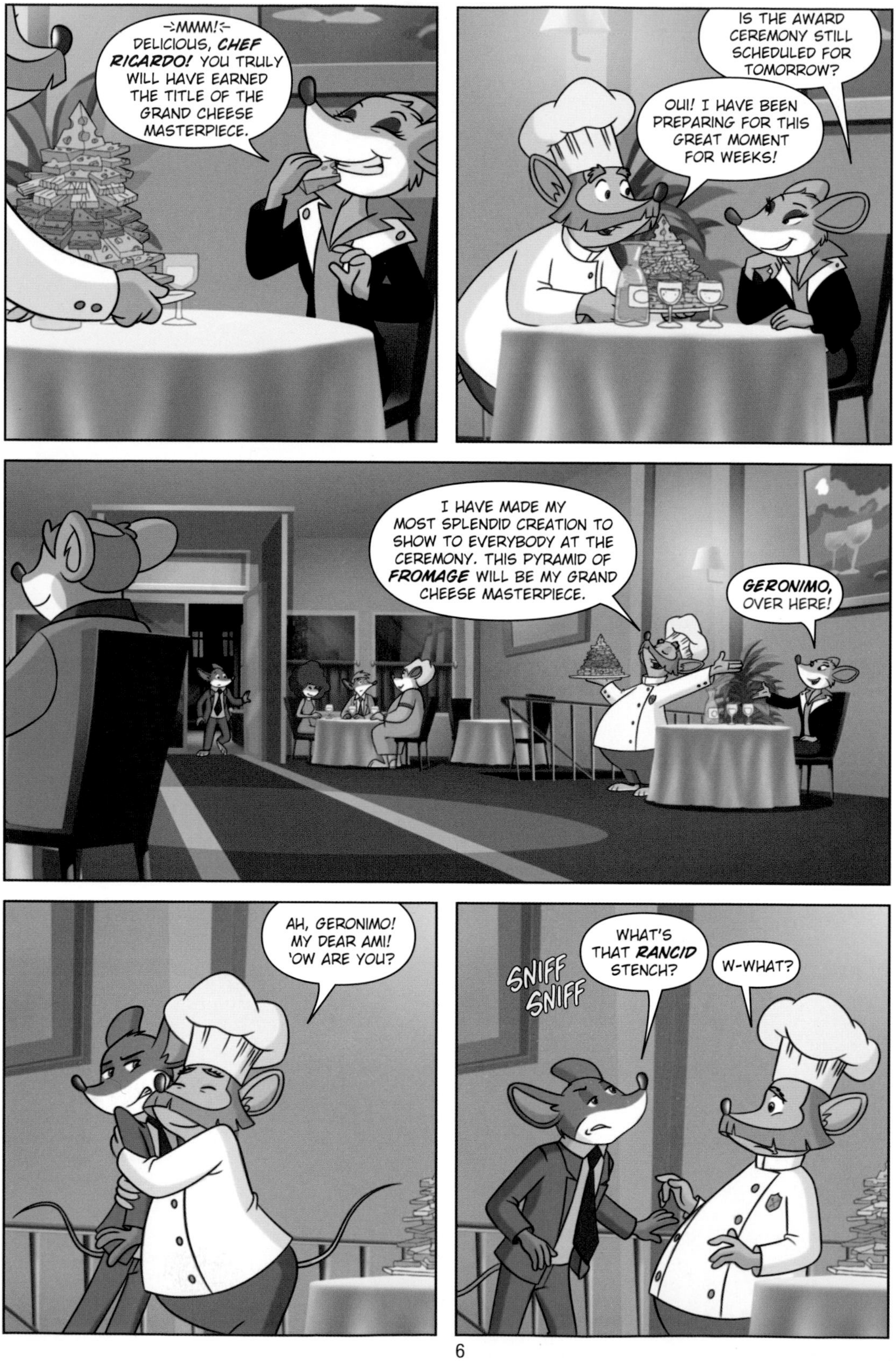
-MMM!- DELICIOUS, CHEF RICARDO! YOU TRULY WILL HAVE EARNED THE TITLE OF THE GRAND CHEESE MASTERPIECE.
IS THE AWARD CEREMONY STILL SCHEDULED FOR TOMORROW?
OUI! I HAVE BEEN PREPARING FOR THIS GREAT MOMENT FOR WEEKS!
I HAVE MADE MY MOST SPLENDID CREATION TO SHOW TO EVERYBODY AT THE CEREMONY. THIS PYRAMID OF FROMAGE WILL BE MY GRAND CHEESE MASTERPIECE.
GERONIMO, OVER HERE!
AH, GERONIMO! MY DEAR AMI! 'OW ARE YOU?
SNIFF SNIFF
WHAT'S THAT RANCID STENCH?
W-WHAT?

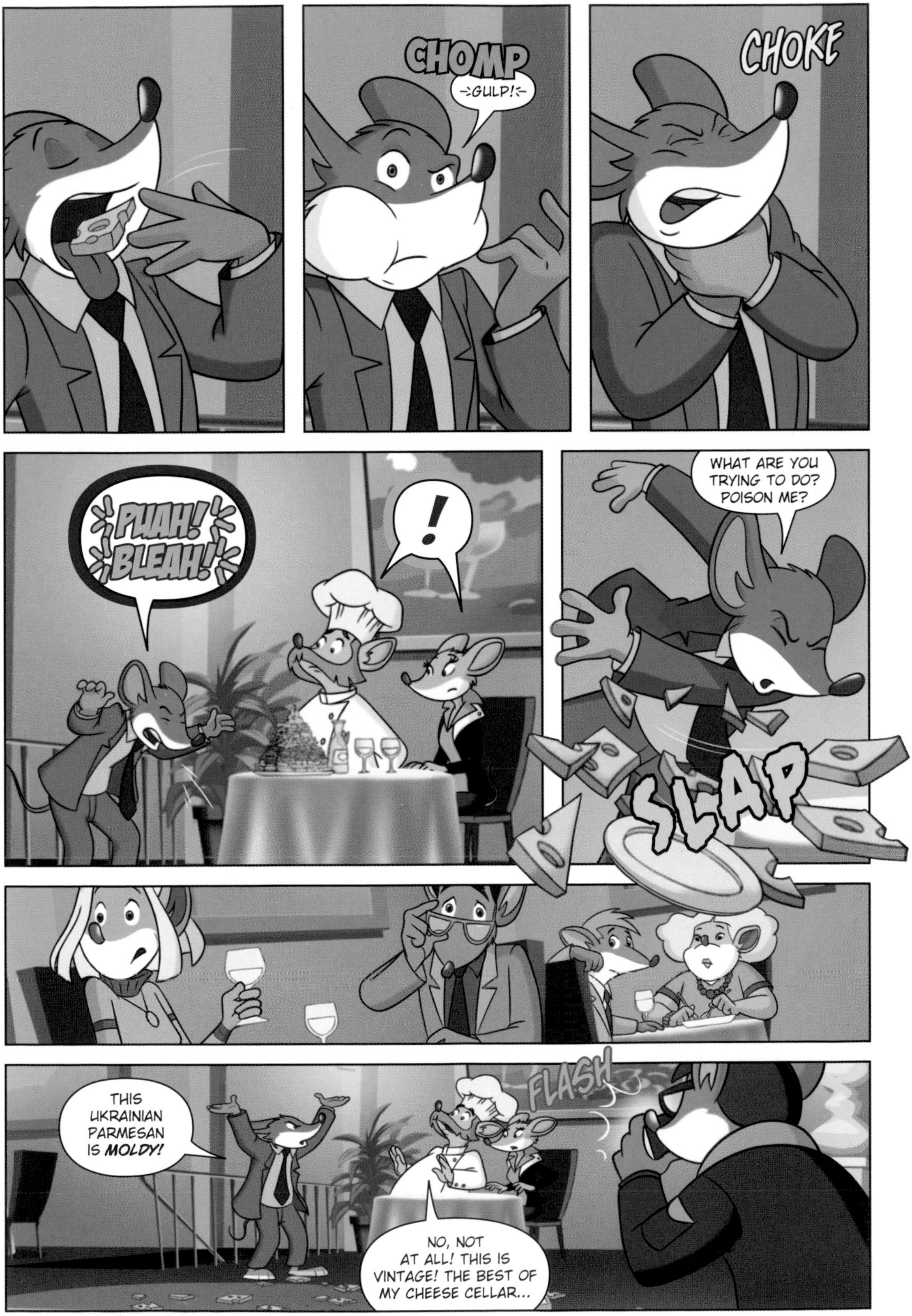

CHOMP
GULP!
CHOKE
PUAH! BLEAH!
!
WHAT ARE YOU TRYING TO DO? POISON ME?
SLAP
THIS UKRAINIAN PARMESAN IS **MOLDY!**
FLASH
NO, NOT AT ALL! THIS IS VINTAGE! THE BEST OF MY CHEESE CELLAR...

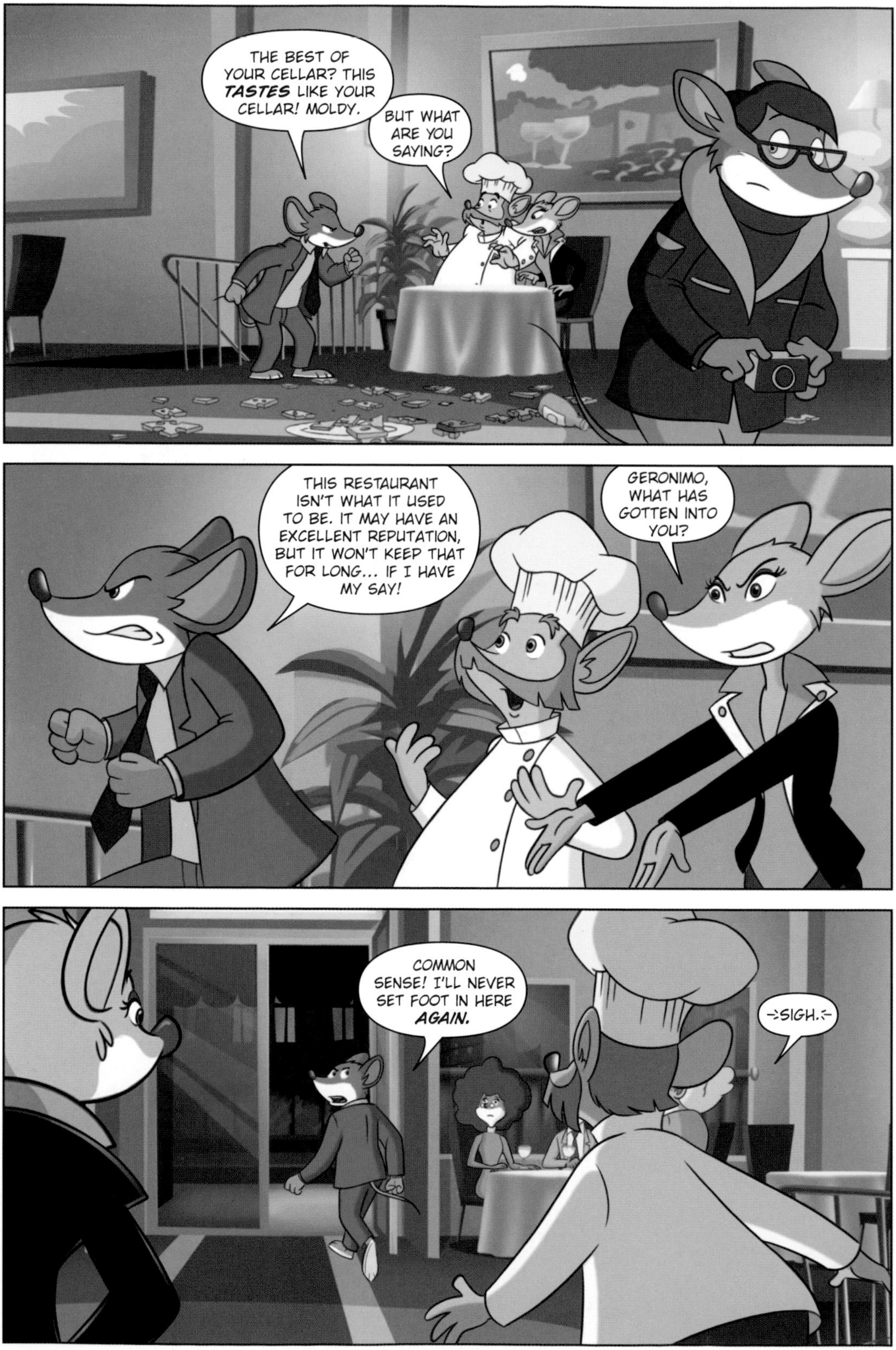
THE BEST OF YOUR CELLAR? THIS TASTES LIKE YOUR CELLAR! MOLDY.
BUT WHAT ARE YOU SAYING?
THIS RESTAURANT ISN'T WHAT IT USED TO BE. IT MAY HAVE AN EXCELLENT REPUTATION, BUT IT WON'T KEEP THAT FOR LONG... IF I HAVE MY SAY!
GERONIMO, WHAT HAS GOTTEN INTO YOU?
COMMON SENSE! I'LL NEVER SET FOOT IN HERE AGAIN.
SIGH.

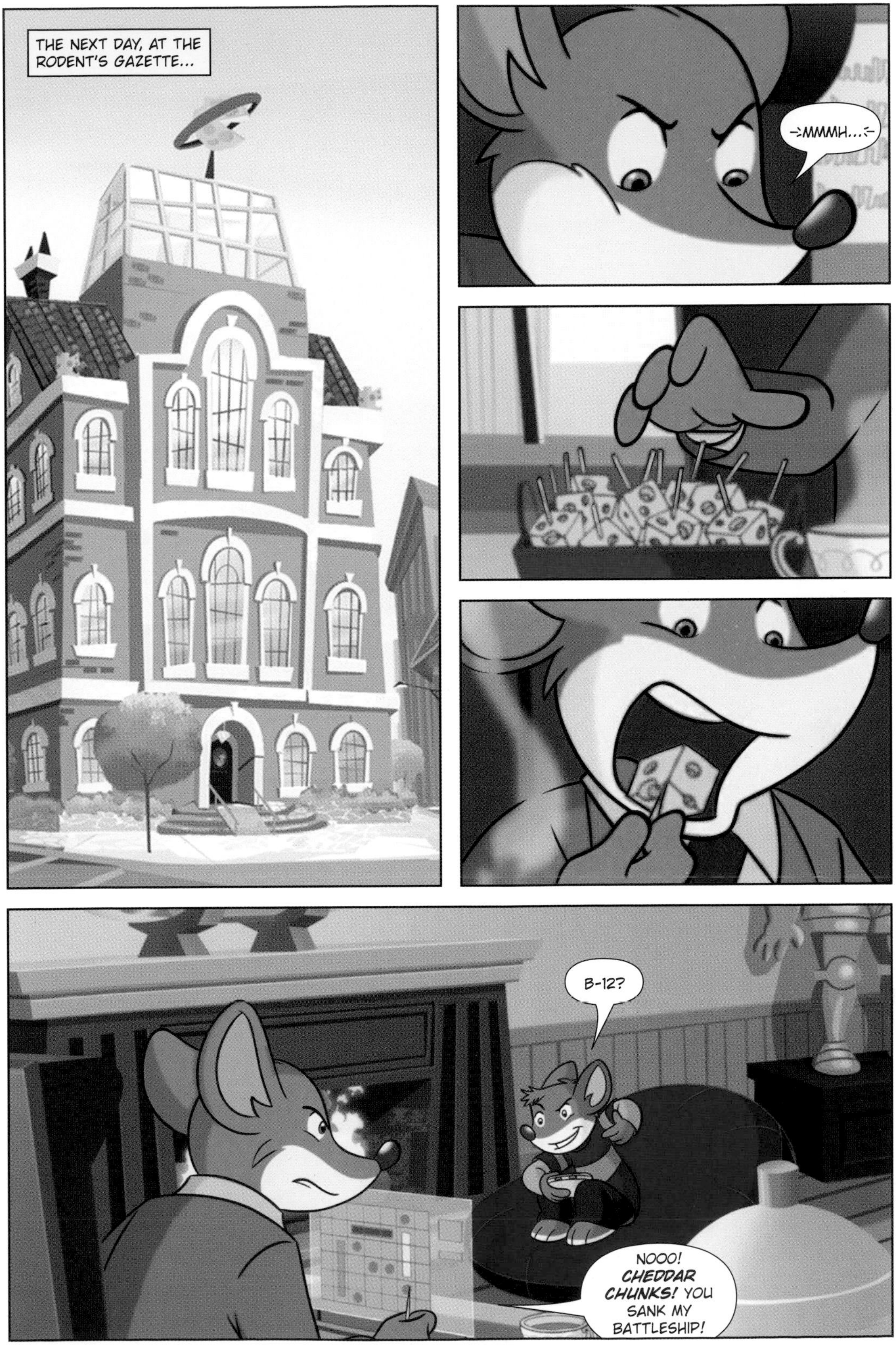
THE NEXT DAY, AT THE RODENT'S GAZETTE...
MMMH...
B-12?
NOOO! CHEDDAR CHUNKS! YOU SANK MY BATTLESHIP!

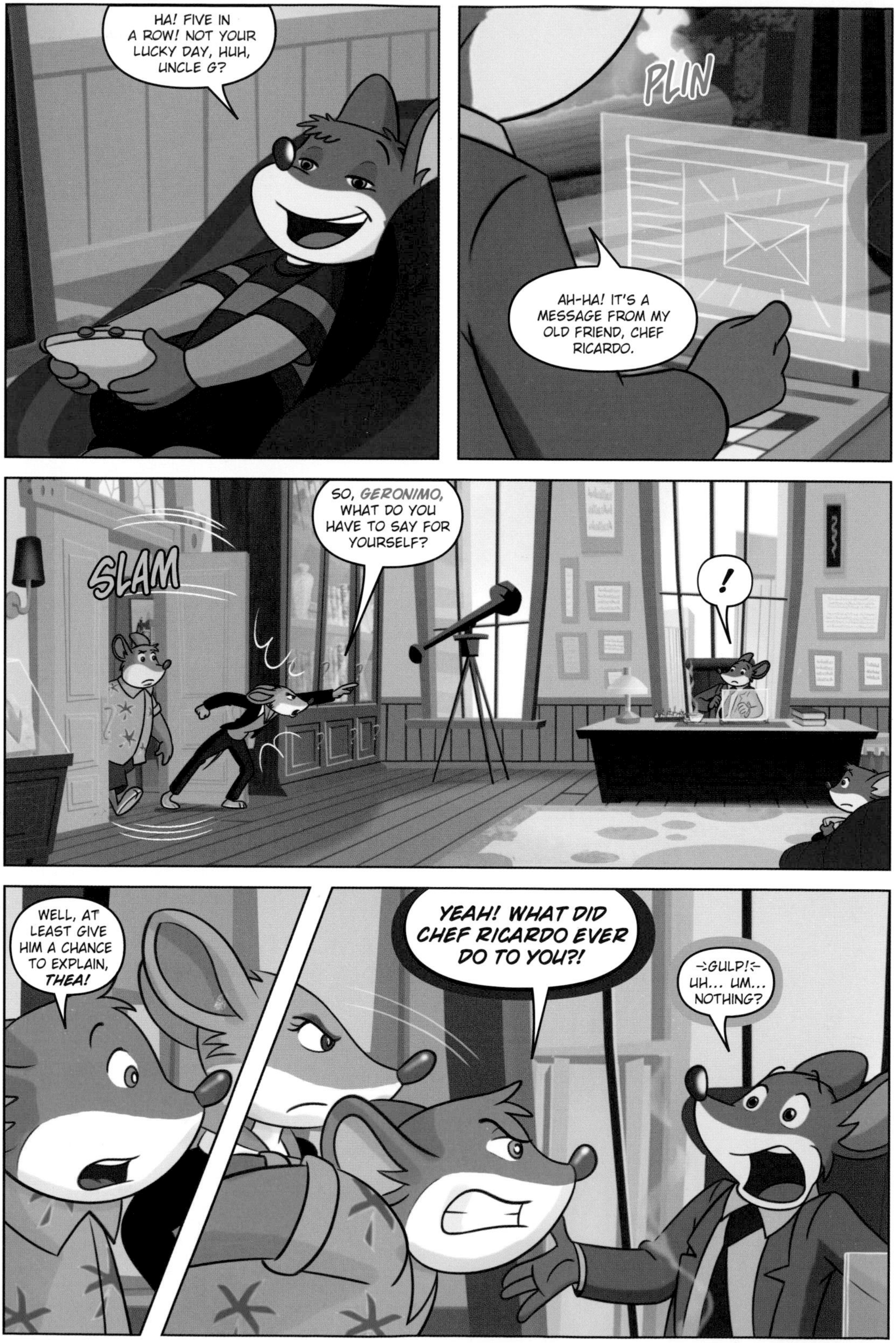

HA! FIVE IN A ROW! NOT YOUR LUCKY DAY, HUH, UNCLE G?
PLIN
AH-HA! IT'S A MESSAGE FROM MY OLD FRIEND, CHEF RICARDO.
SLAM
SO, GERONIMO, WHAT DO YOU HAVE TO SAY FOR YOURSELF?
!
WELL, AT LEAST GIVE HIM A CHANCE TO EXPLAIN, THEA!
YEAH! WHAT DID CHEF RICARDO EVER DO TO YOU?!
GULP! UH... UM... NOTHING?

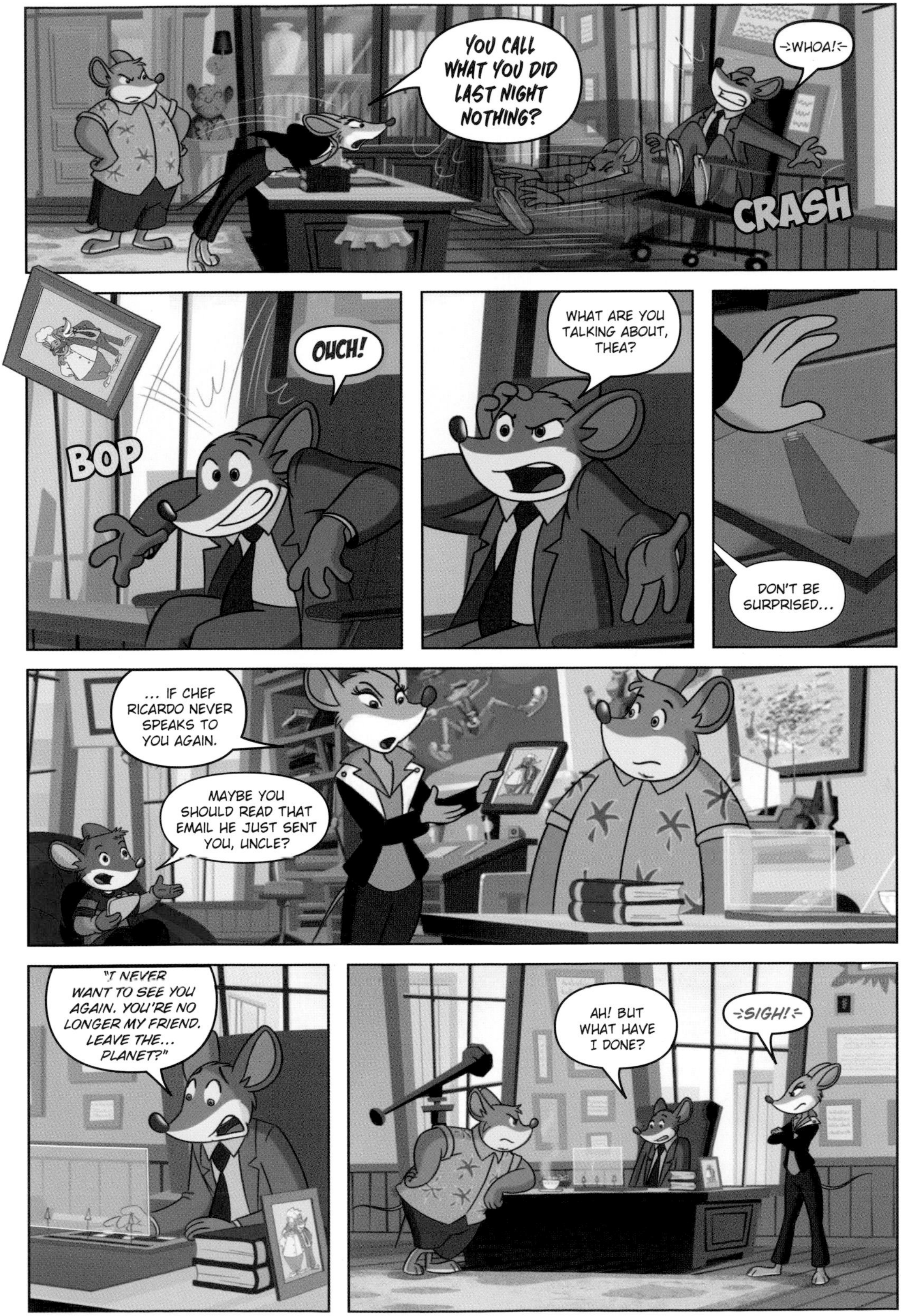
YOU CALL WHAT YOU DID LAST NIGHT NOTHING?
WHOA!
CRASH
OUCH!
BOP
WHAT ARE YOU TALKING ABOUT, THEA?
DON'T BE SURPRISED...
... IF CHEF RICARDO NEVER SPEAKS TO YOU AGAIN.
MAYBE YOU SHOULD READ THAT EMAIL HE JUST SENT YOU, UNCLE?
"I NEVER WANT TO SEE YOU AGAIN. YOU'RE NO LONGER MY FRIEND. LEAVE THE... PLANET?"
AH! BUT WHAT HAVE I DONE?
SIGH!

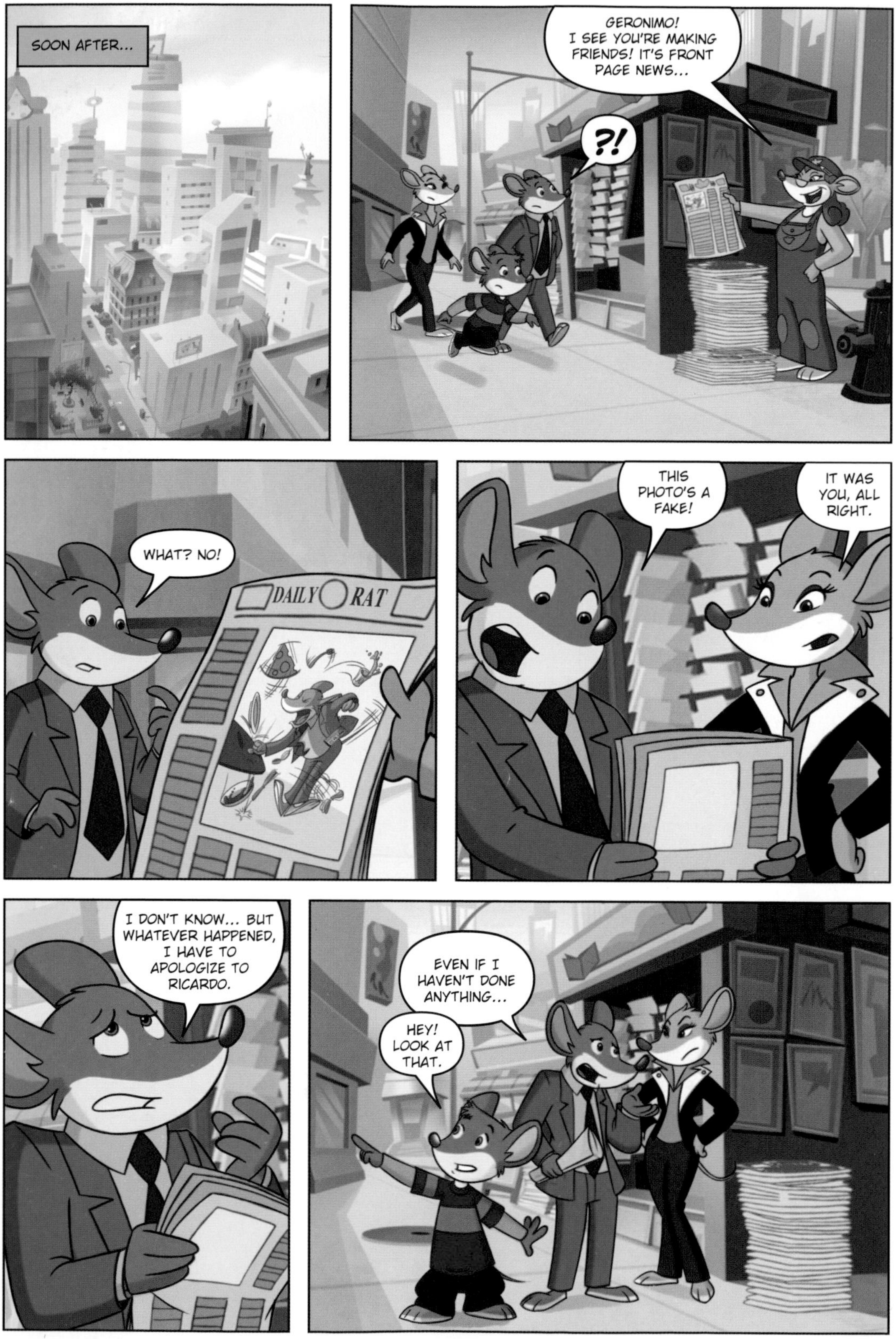

SOON AFTER...
GERONIMO! I SEE YOU'RE MAKING FRIENDS! IT'S FRONT PAGE NEWS...
?!
WHAT? NO!
DAILY RAT
THIS PHOTO'S A FAKE!
IT WAS YOU, ALL RIGHT.
I DON'T KNOW... BUT WHATEVER HAPPENED, I HAVE TO APOLOGIZE TO RICARDO.
EVEN IF I HAVEN'T DONE ANYTHING...
HEY! LOOK AT THAT.

IT'S *TRUFFOLON!*

OOOH, NORDIC TRIPLE-CREAM TRUFFOLON. EXTREMELY RARE CHEESE... CREAMY, YET SHARP, WITH A SASSY SLAP OF MINT.

NOT A BAD WAY TO APOLOGIZE TO A FRIEND, HUH? HEY, UNCLE G?

BENJAMIN, YOU'RE RIGHT.

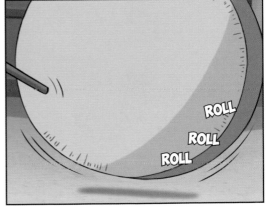

ROLL

ROLL

ROLL

YOU'RE SERIOUS ABOUT THIS?

I HOPE HE LIKES IT.

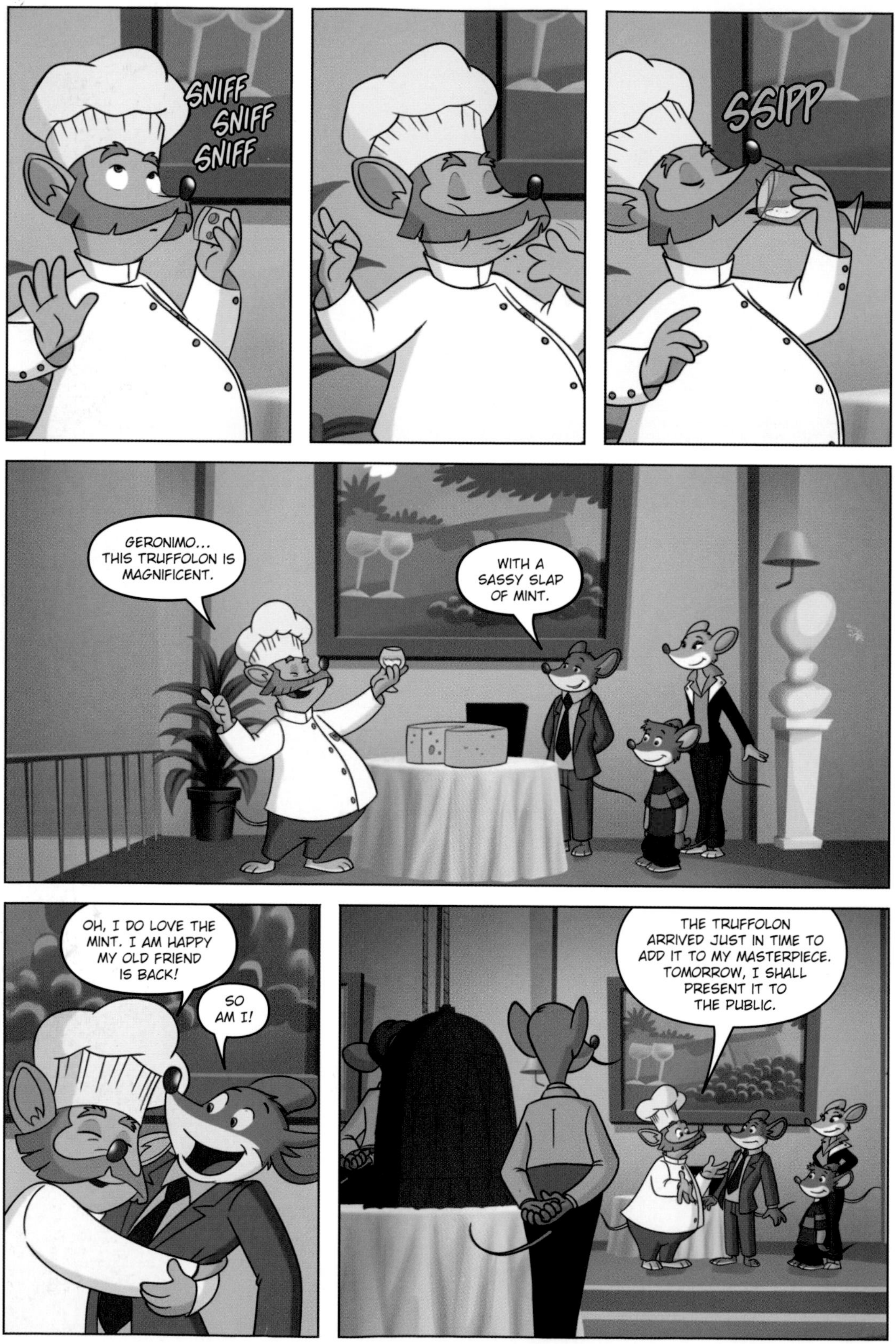
SNIFF
SNIFF
SNIFF
SSIPP
GERONIMO... THIS TRUFFOLON IS MAGNIFICENT.
WITH A SASSY SLAP OF MINT.
OH, I DO LOVE THE MINT. I AM HAPPY MY OLD FRIEND IS BACK!
SO AM I!
THE TRUFFOLON ARRIVED JUST IN TIME TO ADD IT TO MY MASTERPIECE. TOMORROW, I SHALL PRESENT IT TO THE PUBLIC.

OOOOH!

I WOULD LOVE IF THE RODENT'S GAZETTTE WOULD COVER THE EVENT.

I WOULD BE VERY HONORED.

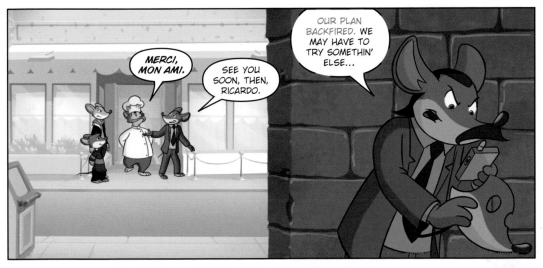

MERCI, MON AMI.

SEE YOU SOON, THEN, RICARDO.

OUR PLAN BACKFIRED. WE MAY HAVE TO TRY SOMETHIN' ELSE...

RUSTLE RUSTLE RUSTLE

HEH HEH HEH

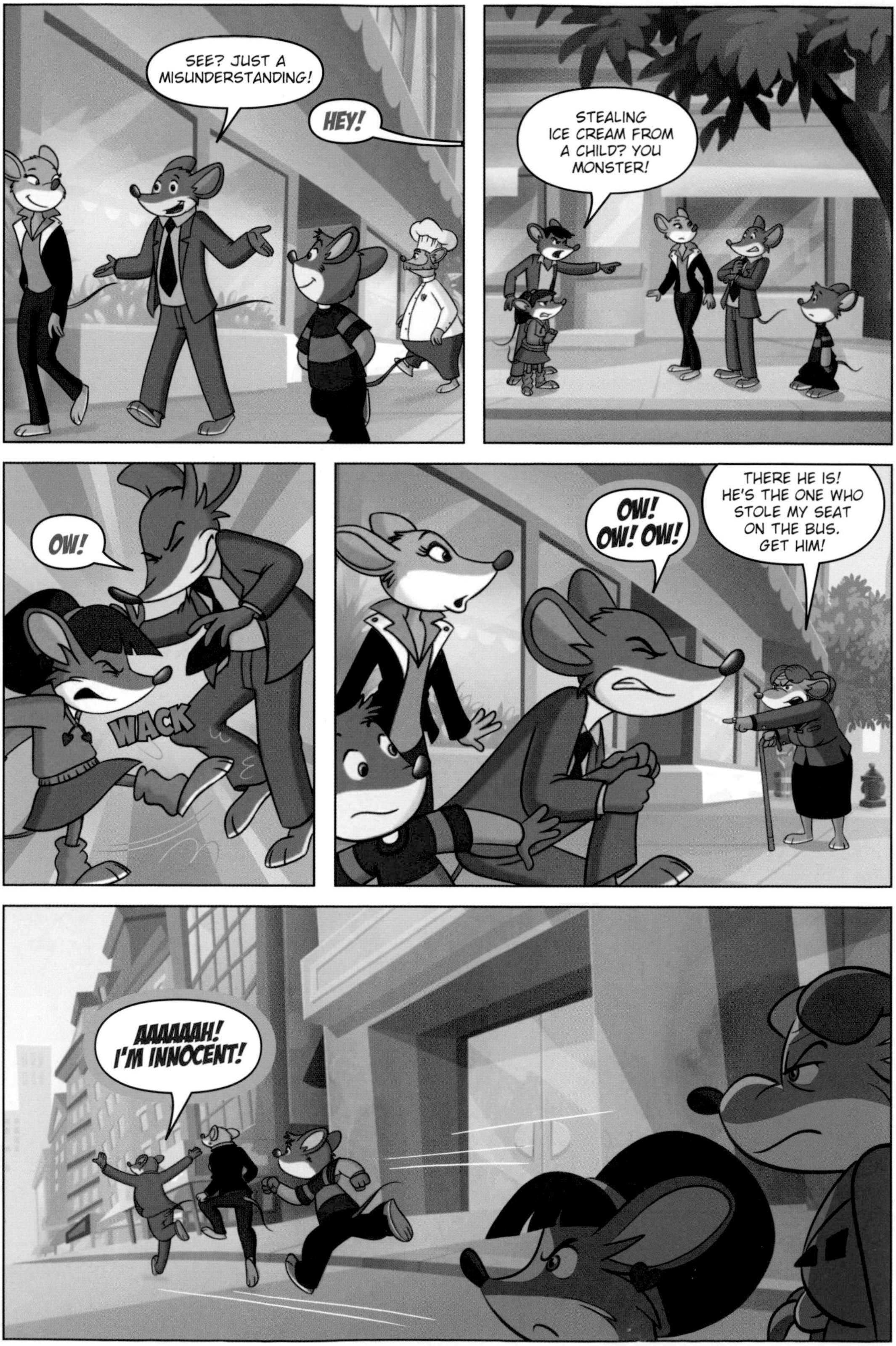
SEE? JUST A MISUNDERSTANDING!
HEY!
STEALING ICE CREAM FROM A CHILD? YOU MONSTER!
OW!
WACK
OW! OW! OW!
THERE HE IS! HE'S THE ONE WHO STOLE MY SEAT ON THE BUS. GET HIM!
AAAAAAH! I'M INNOCENT!

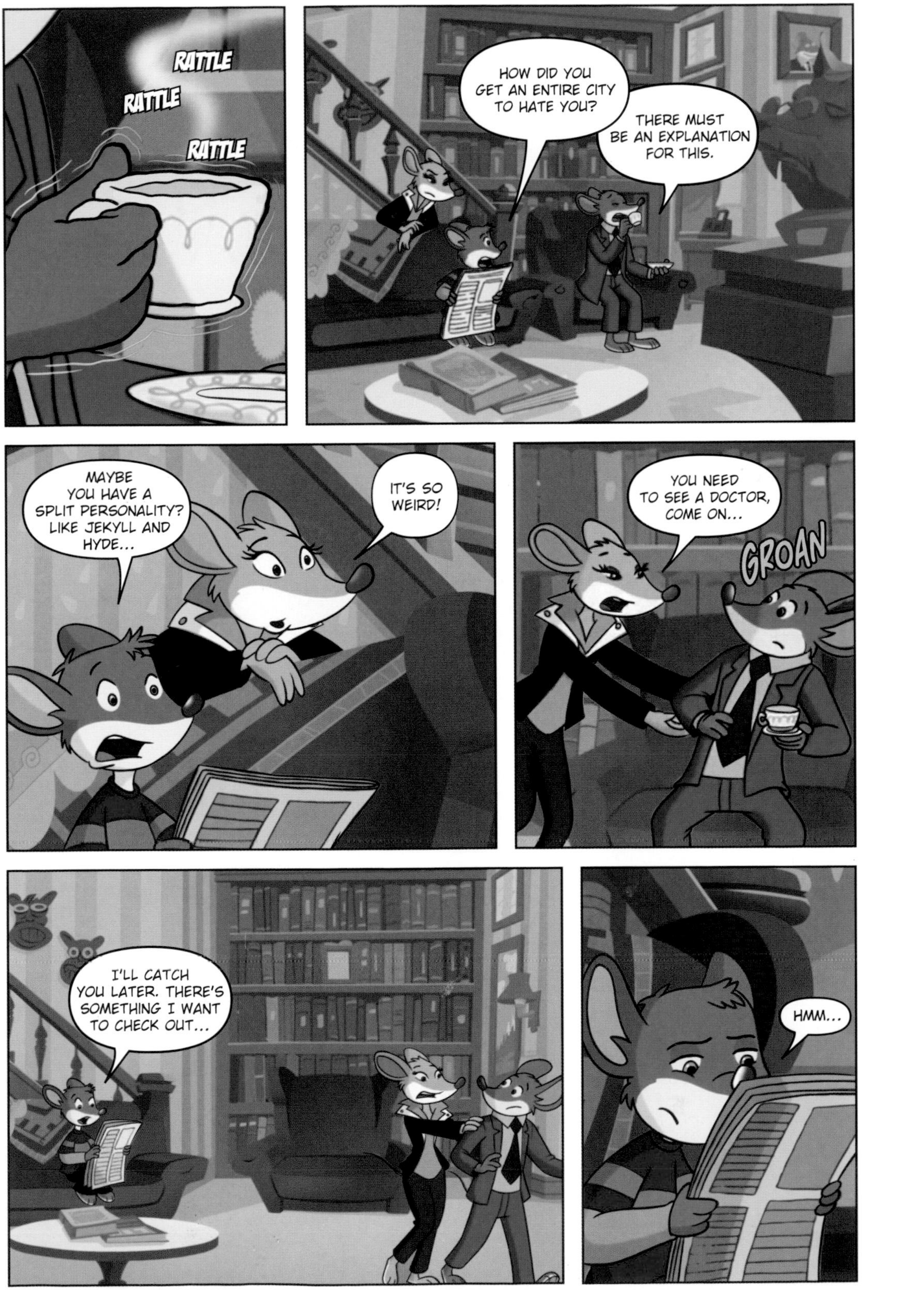
RATTLE
RATTLE
RATTLE
HOW DID YOU GET AN ENTIRE CITY TO HATE YOU?
THERE MUST BE AN EXPLANATION FOR THIS.
MAYBE YOU HAVE A SPLIT PERSONALITY? LIKE JEKYLL AND HYDE...
IT'S SO WEIRD!
YOU NEED TO SEE A DOCTOR, COME ON...
GROAN
I'LL CATCH YOU LATER. THERE'S SOMETHING I WANT TO CHECK OUT...
HMM...

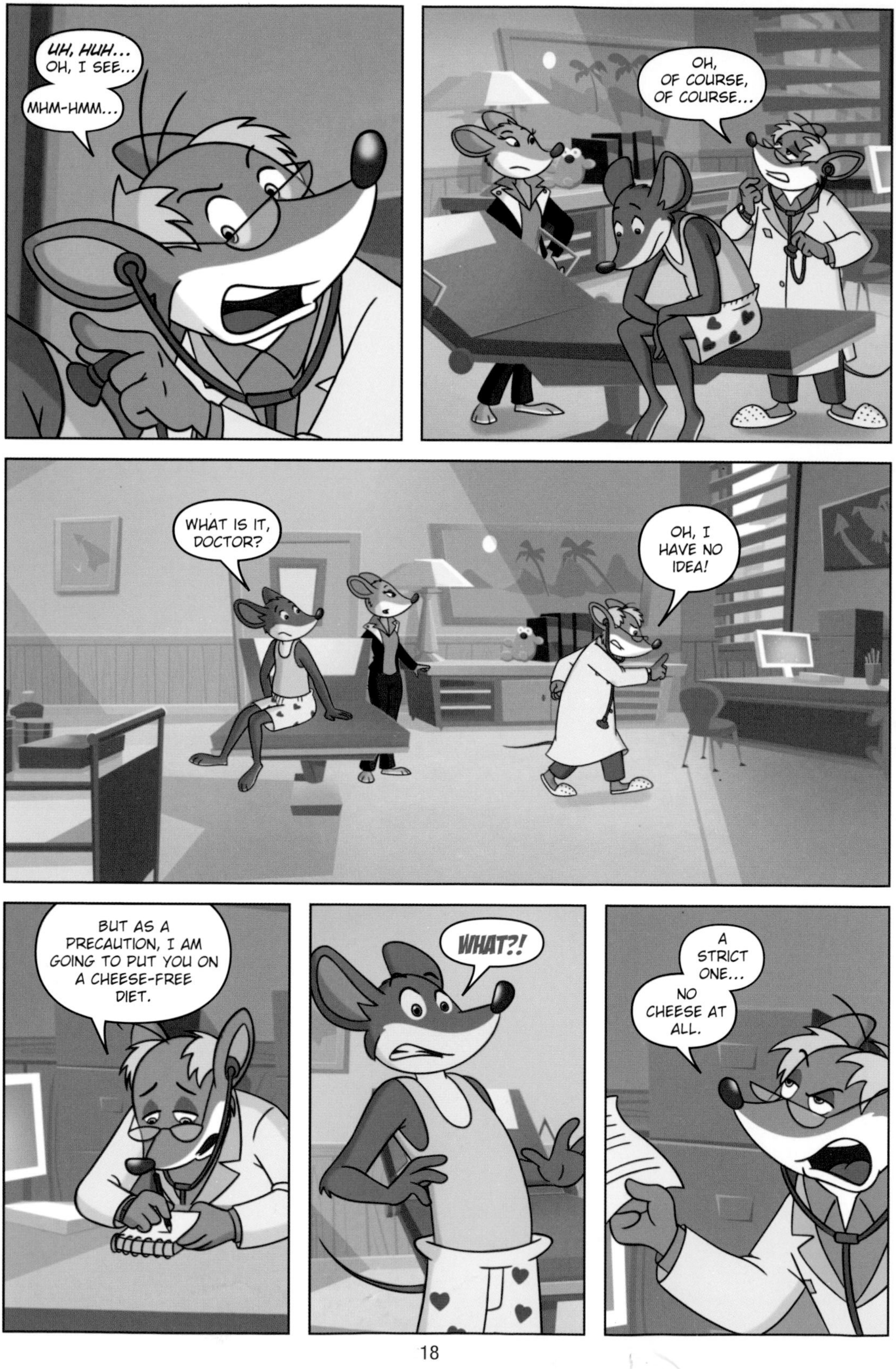
UH, HUH... OH, I SEE...
MHM-HMM...
OH, OF COURSE, OF COURSE...
WHAT IS IT, DOCTOR?
OH, I HAVE NO IDEA!
BUT AS A PRECAUTION, I AM GOING TO PUT YOU ON A CHEESE-FREE DIET.
WHAT?!
A STRICT ONE...
NO CHEESE AT ALL.

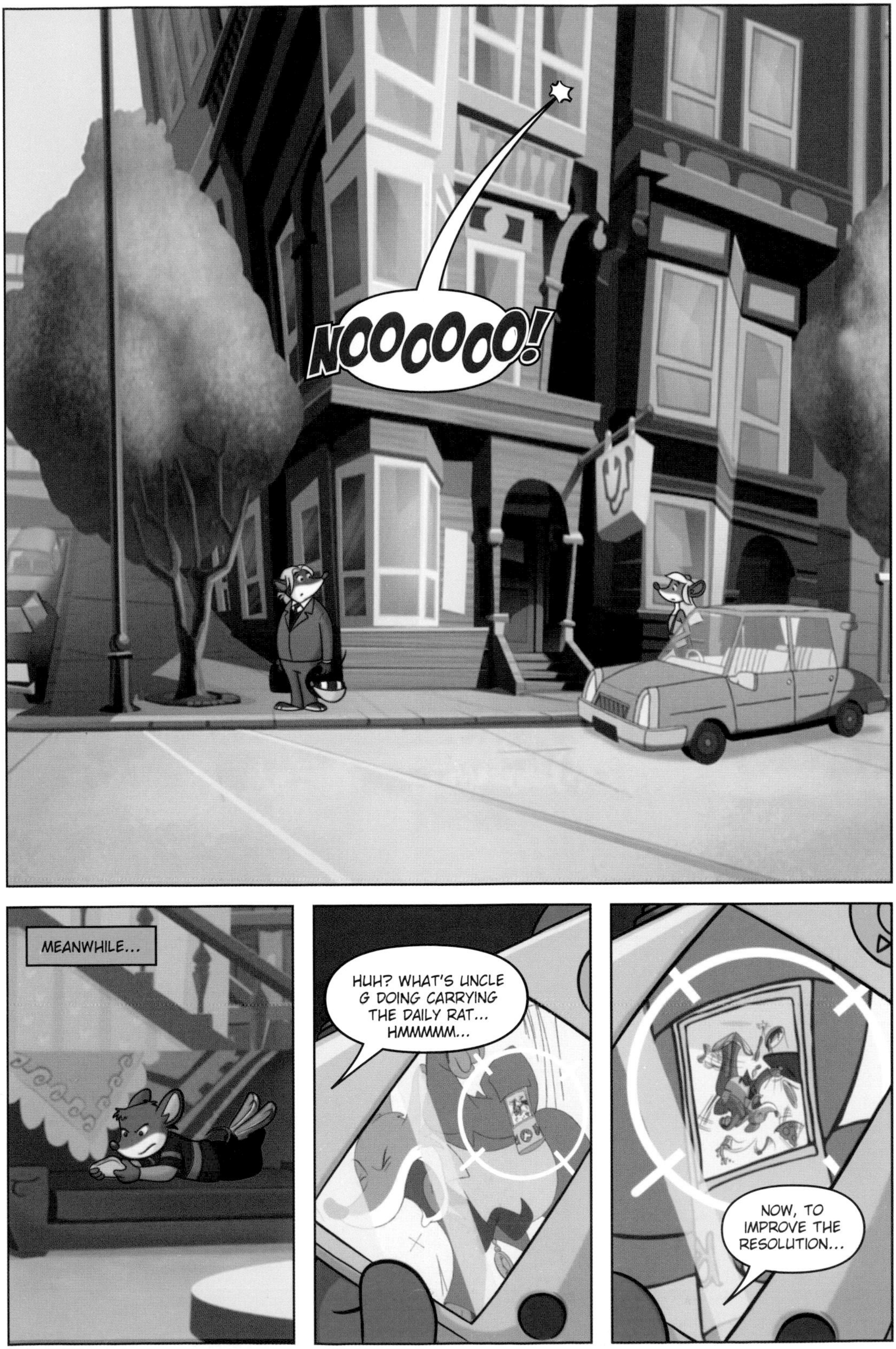
NOOOOOO!
MEANWHILE...
HUH? WHAT'S UNCLE G DOING CARRYING THE DAILY RAT... HMMMMM...
NOW, TO IMPROVE THE RESOLUTION...

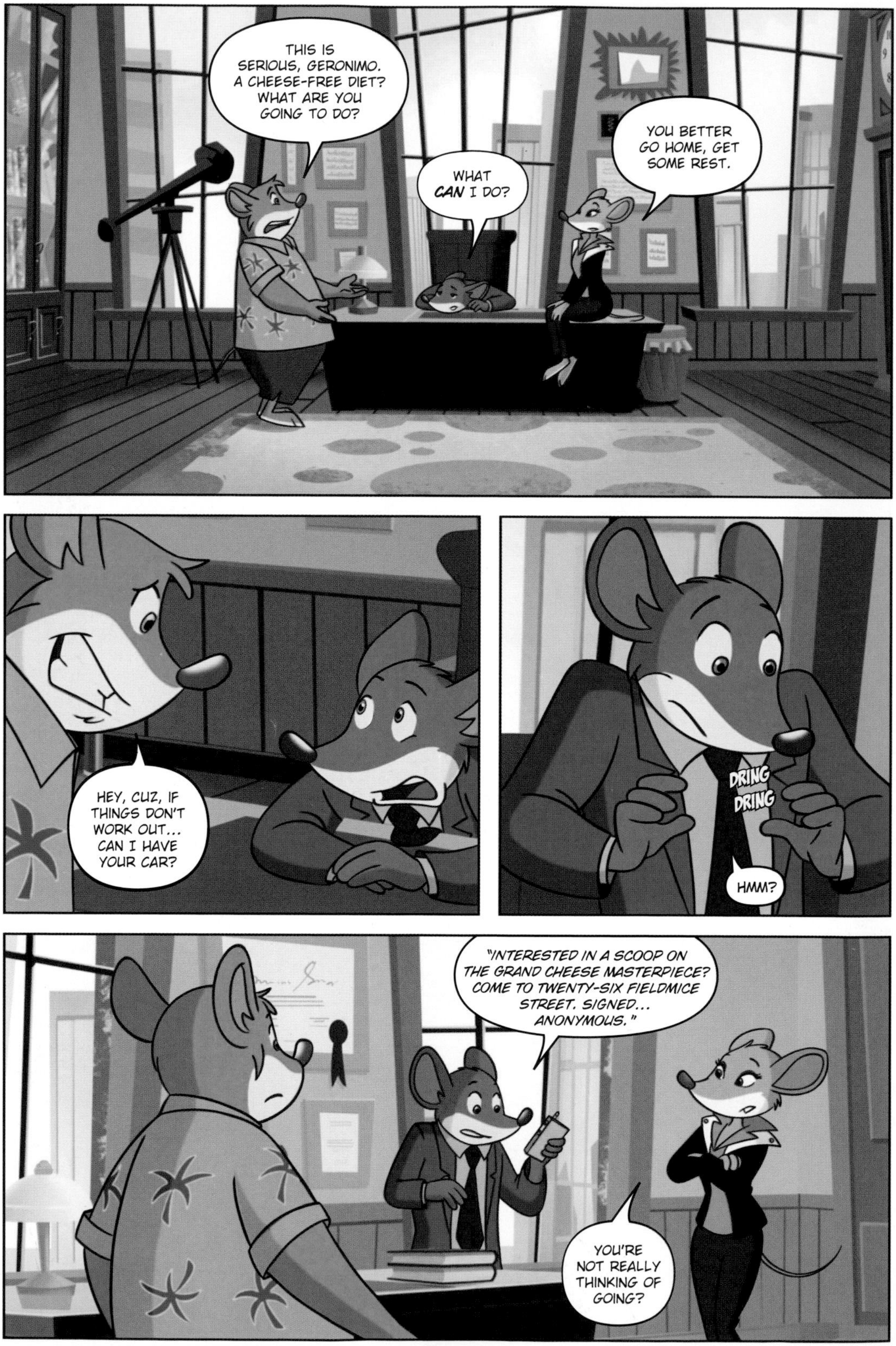
THIS IS SERIOUS, GERONIMO. A CHEESE-FREE DIET? WHAT ARE YOU GOING TO DO?
WHAT CAN I DO?
YOU BETTER GO HOME, GET SOME REST.
HEY, CUZ, IF THINGS DON'T WORK OUT... CAN I HAVE YOUR CAR?
DRING DRING
HMM?
"INTERESTED IN A SCOOP ON THE GRAND CHEESE MASTERPIECE? COME TO TWENTY-SIX FIELDMICE STREET. SIGNED... ANONYMOUS."
YOU'RE NOT REALLY THINKING OF GOING?

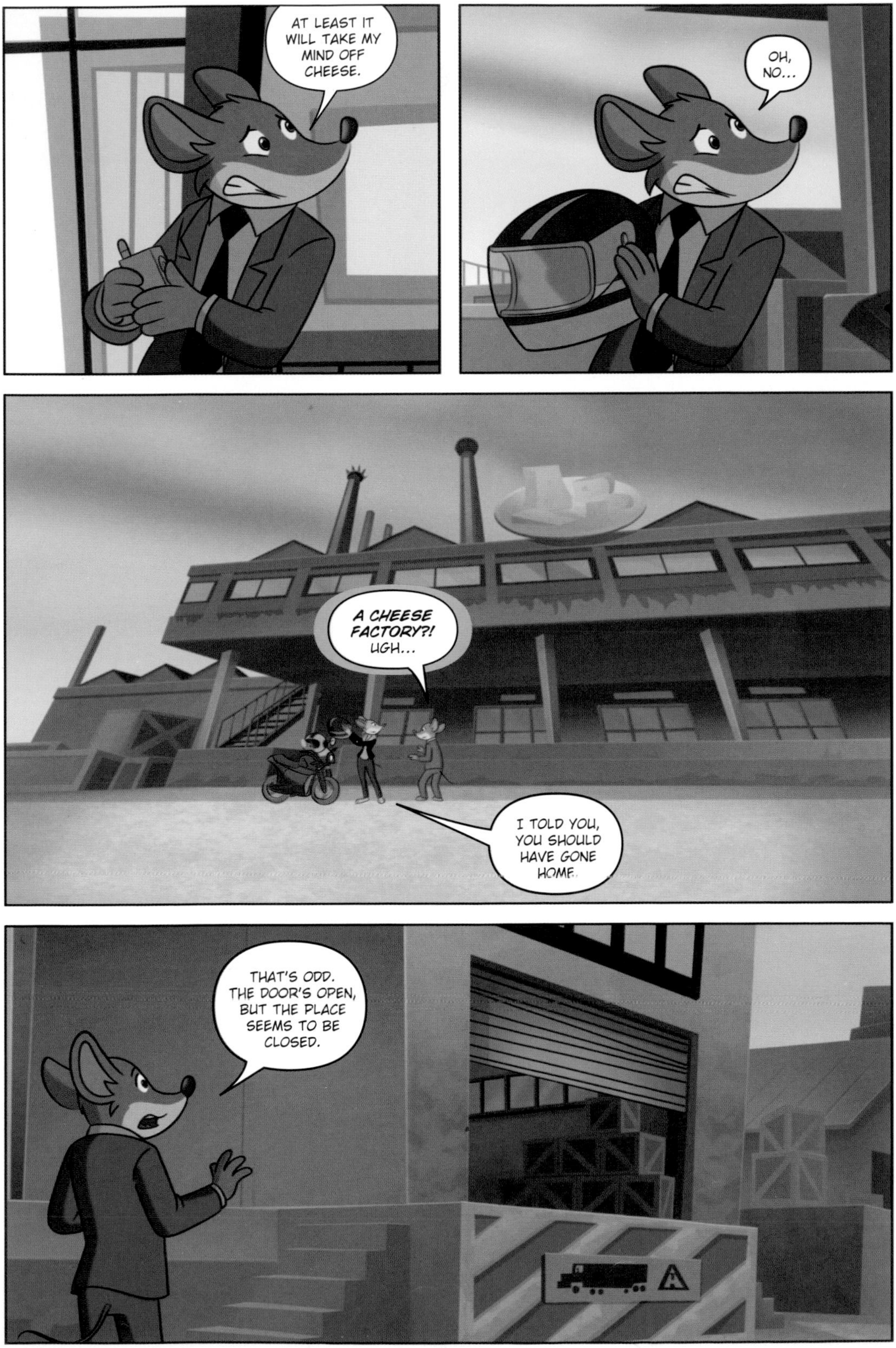
AT LEAST IT WILL TAKE MY MIND OFF CHEESE.
OH, NO...
A CHEESE FACTORY?! UGH...
I TOLD YOU, YOU SHOULD HAVE GONE HOME.
THAT'S ODD. THE DOOR'S OPEN, BUT THE PLACE SEEMS TO BE CLOSED.

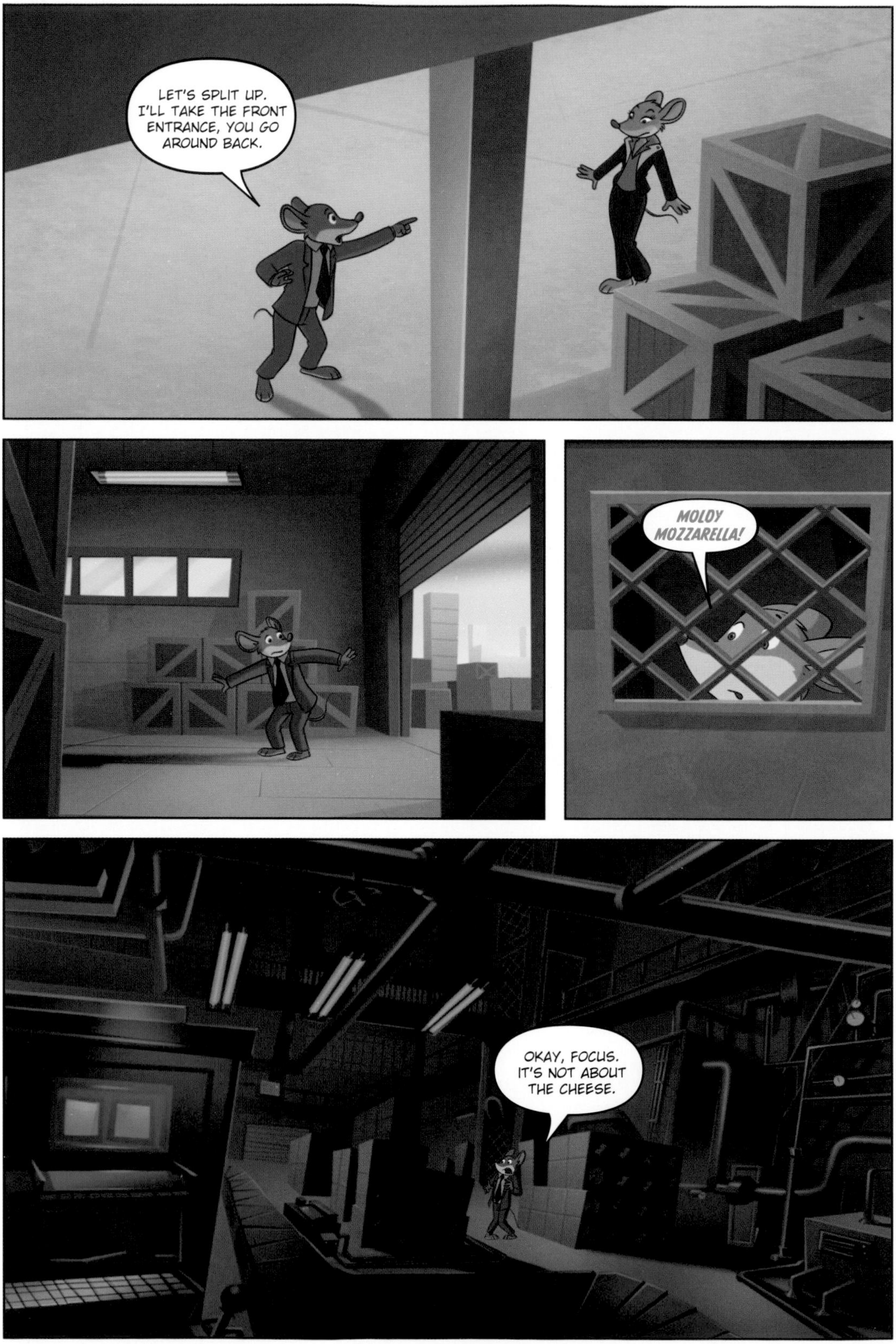
LET'S SPLIT UP. I'LL TAKE THE FRONT ENTRANCE, YOU GO AROUND BACK.
MOLDY MOZZARELLA!
OKAY, FOCUS. IT'S NOT ABOUT THE CHEESE.

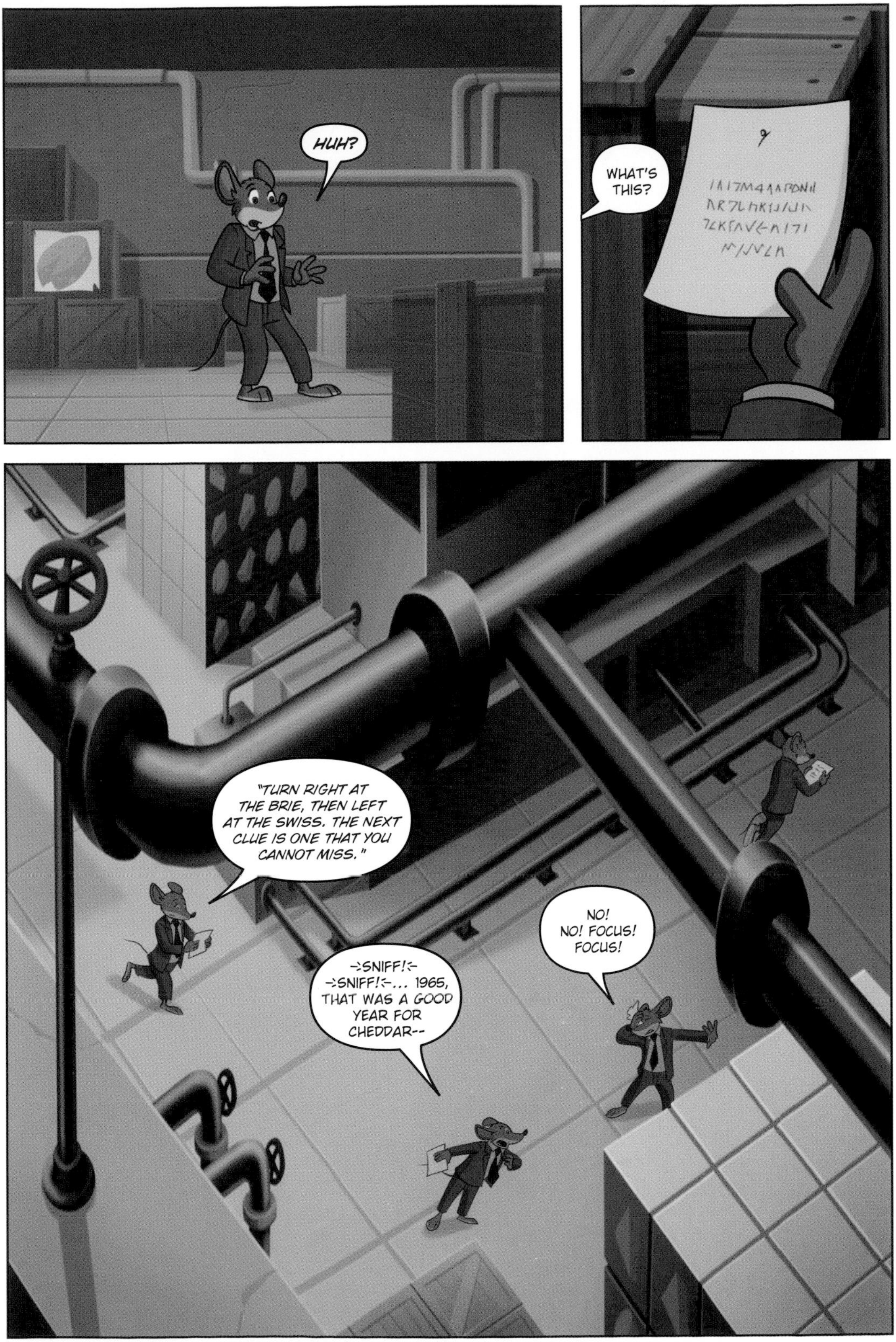
HUH?
WHAT'S THIS?
"TURN RIGHT AT THE BRIE, THEN LEFT AT THE SWISS. THE NEXT CLUE IS ONE THAT YOU CANNOT MISS."
SNIFF! SNIFF!... 1965, THAT WAS A GOOD YEAR FOR CHEDDAR--
NO! NO! FOCUS! FOCUS!

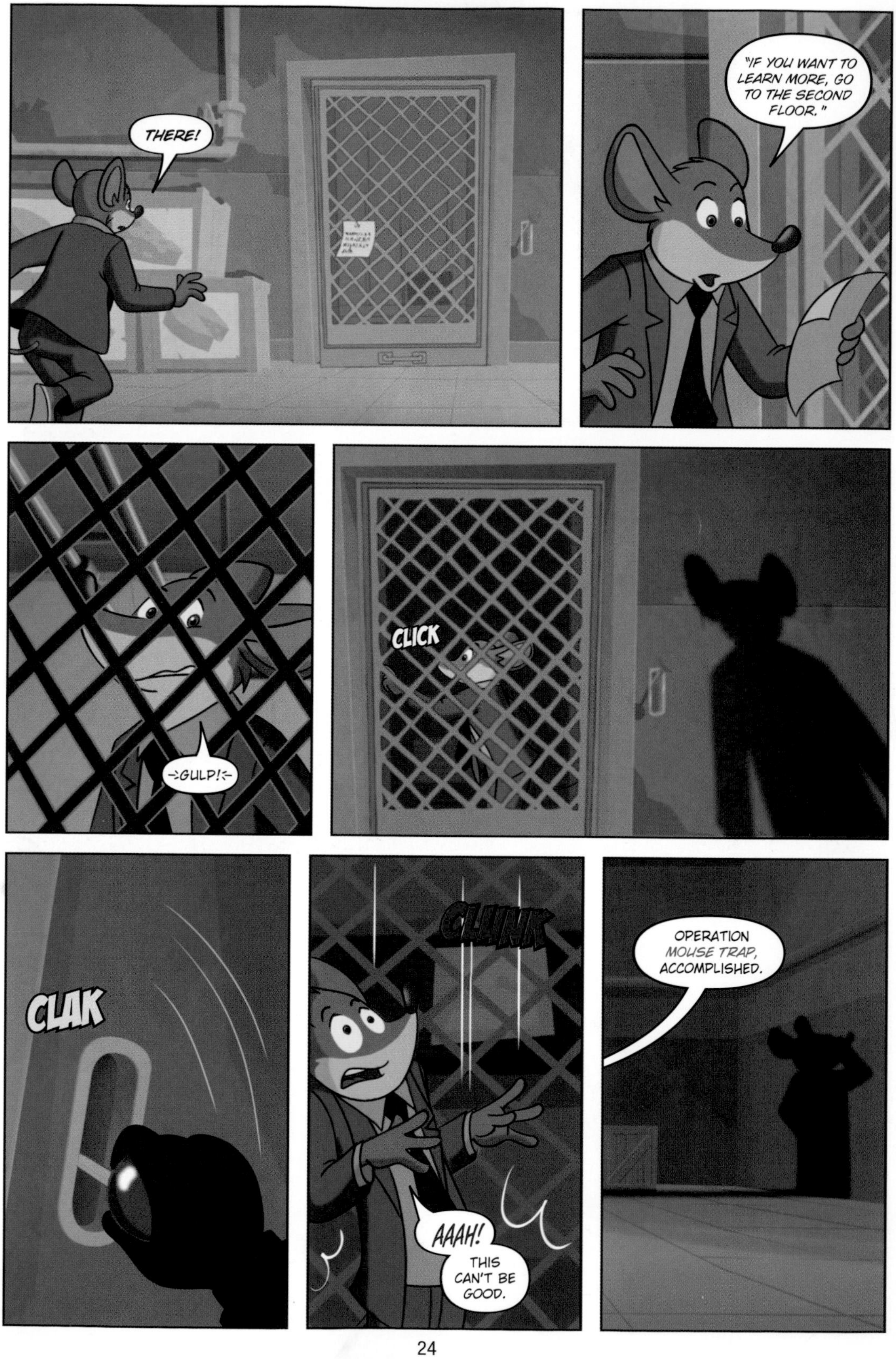
THERE!
"IF YOU WANT TO LEARN MORE, GO TO THE SECOND FLOOR."
-GULP!-
CLICK
CLAK
CLUNK
AAAH! THIS CAN'T BE GOOD.
OPERATION MOUSE TRAP, ACCOMPLISHED.

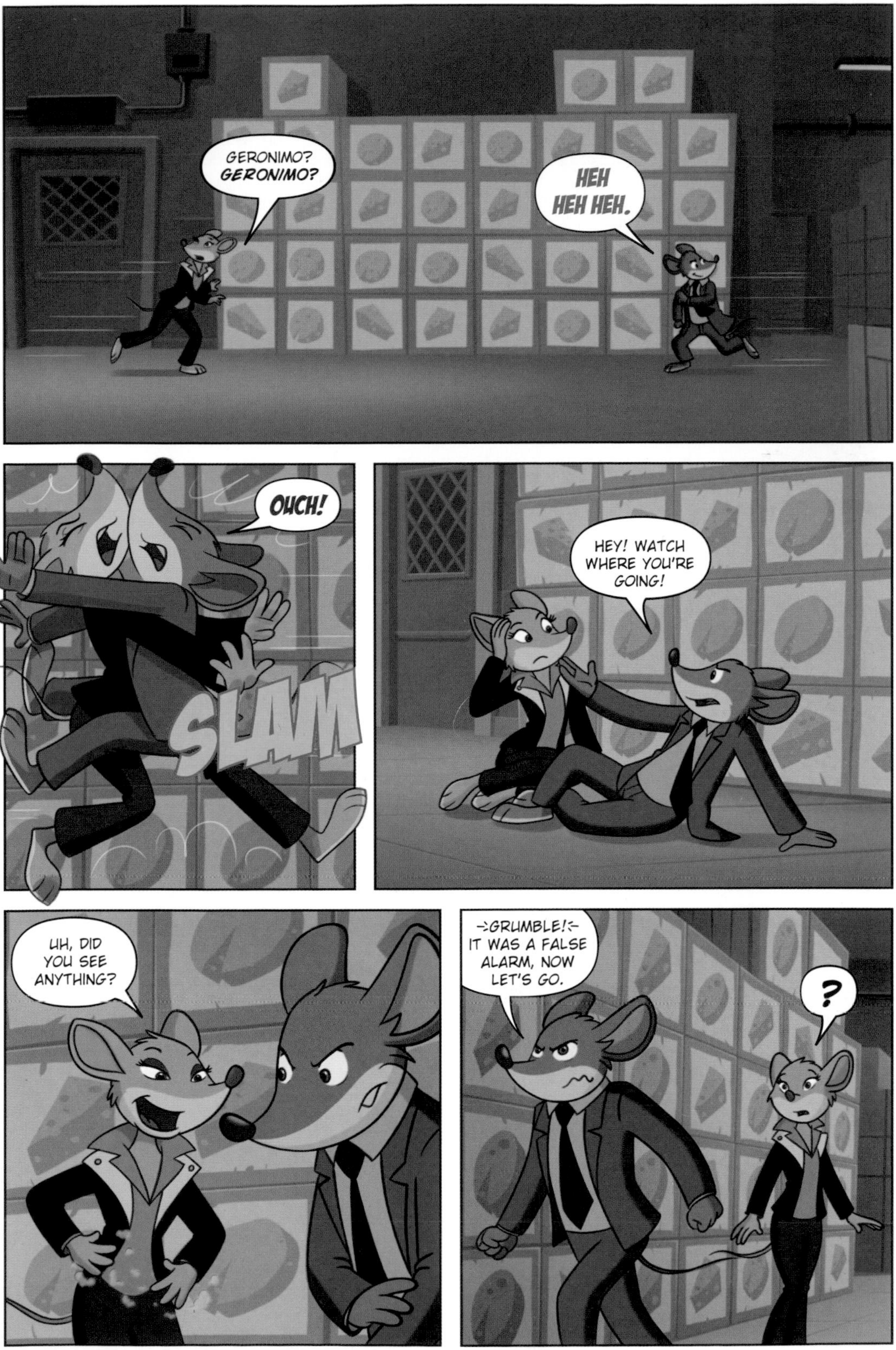
GERONIMO? GERONIMO?
HEH HEH HEH.
OUCH!
SLAM
HEY! WATCH WHERE YOU'RE GOING!
UH, DID YOU SEE ANYTHING?
-GRUMBLE!- IT WAS A FALSE ALARM, NOW LET'S GO.
?

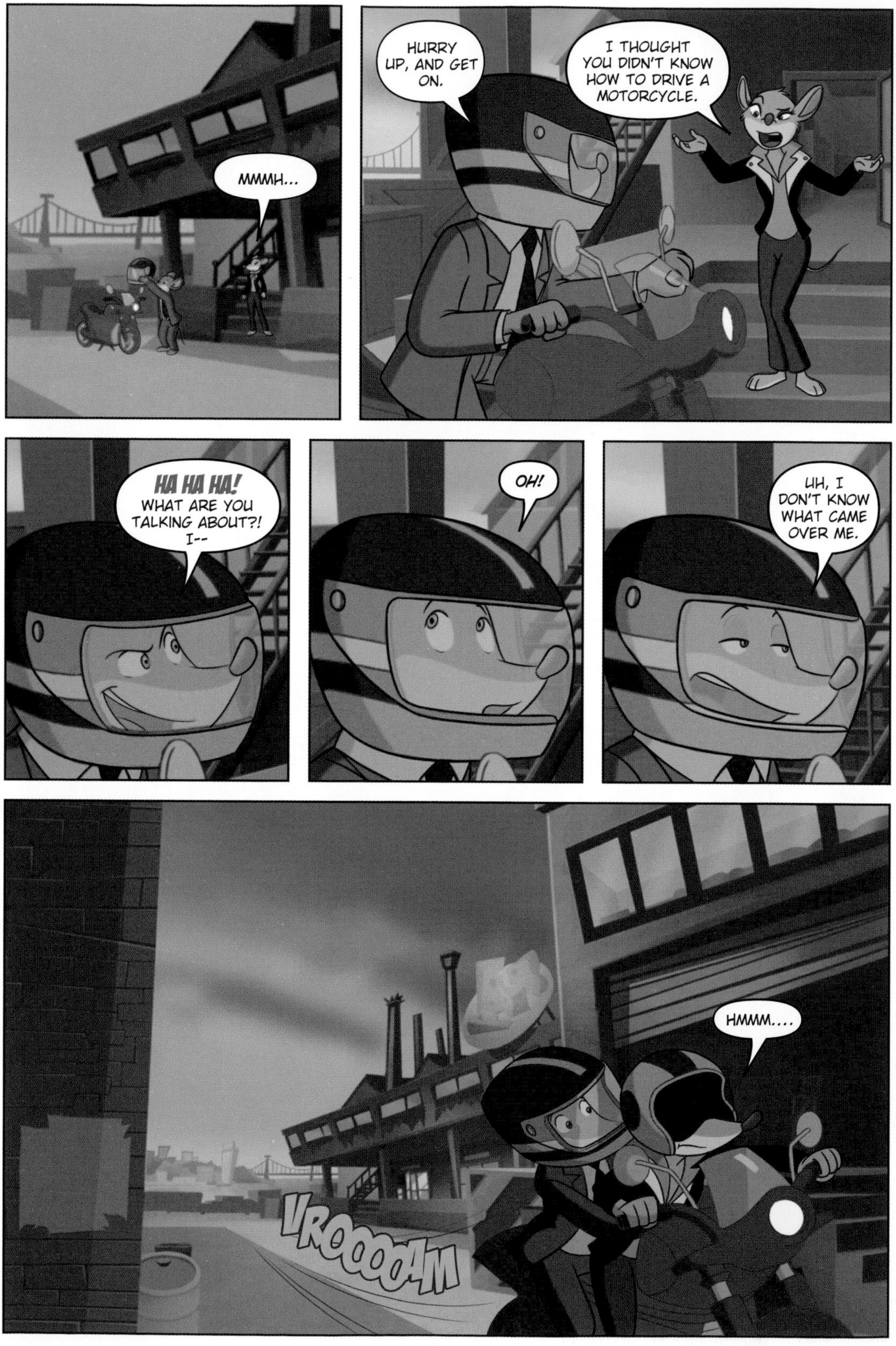
MMMH...
HURRY UP, AND GET ON.
I THOUGHT YOU DIDN'T KNOW HOW TO DRIVE A MOTORCYCLE.
HA HA HA! WHAT ARE YOU TALKING ABOUT?! I--
OH!
UH, I DON'T KNOW WHAT CAME OVER ME.
HMMM....
VROOOOAM

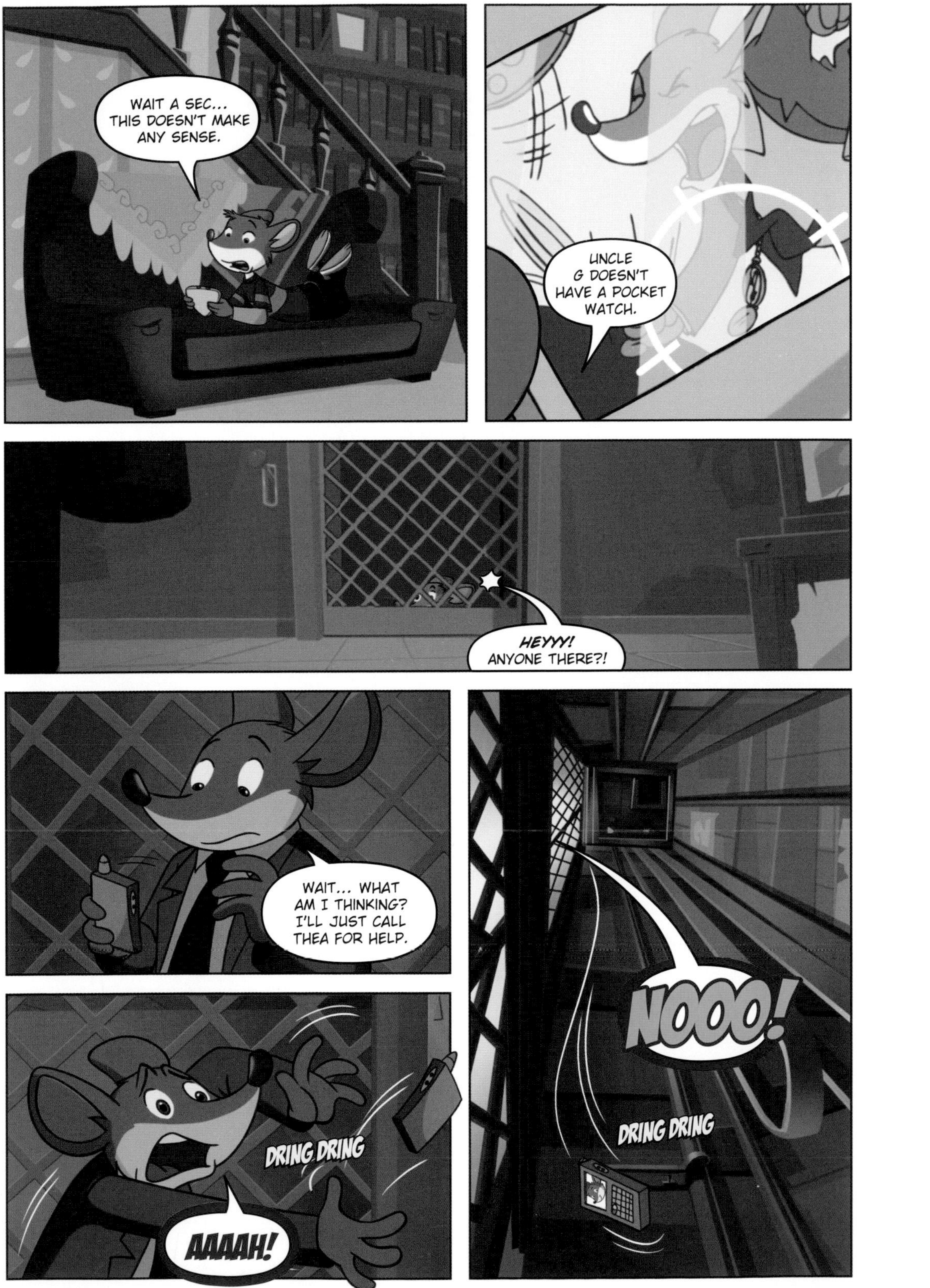
WAIT A SEC... THIS DOESN'T MAKE ANY SENSE.
UNCLE G DOESN'T HAVE A POCKET WATCH.
HEYYY! ANYONE THERE?!
WAIT... WHAT AM I THINKING? I'LL JUST CALL THEA FOR HELP.
DRING DRING
AAAAH!
NOOO!
DRING DRING

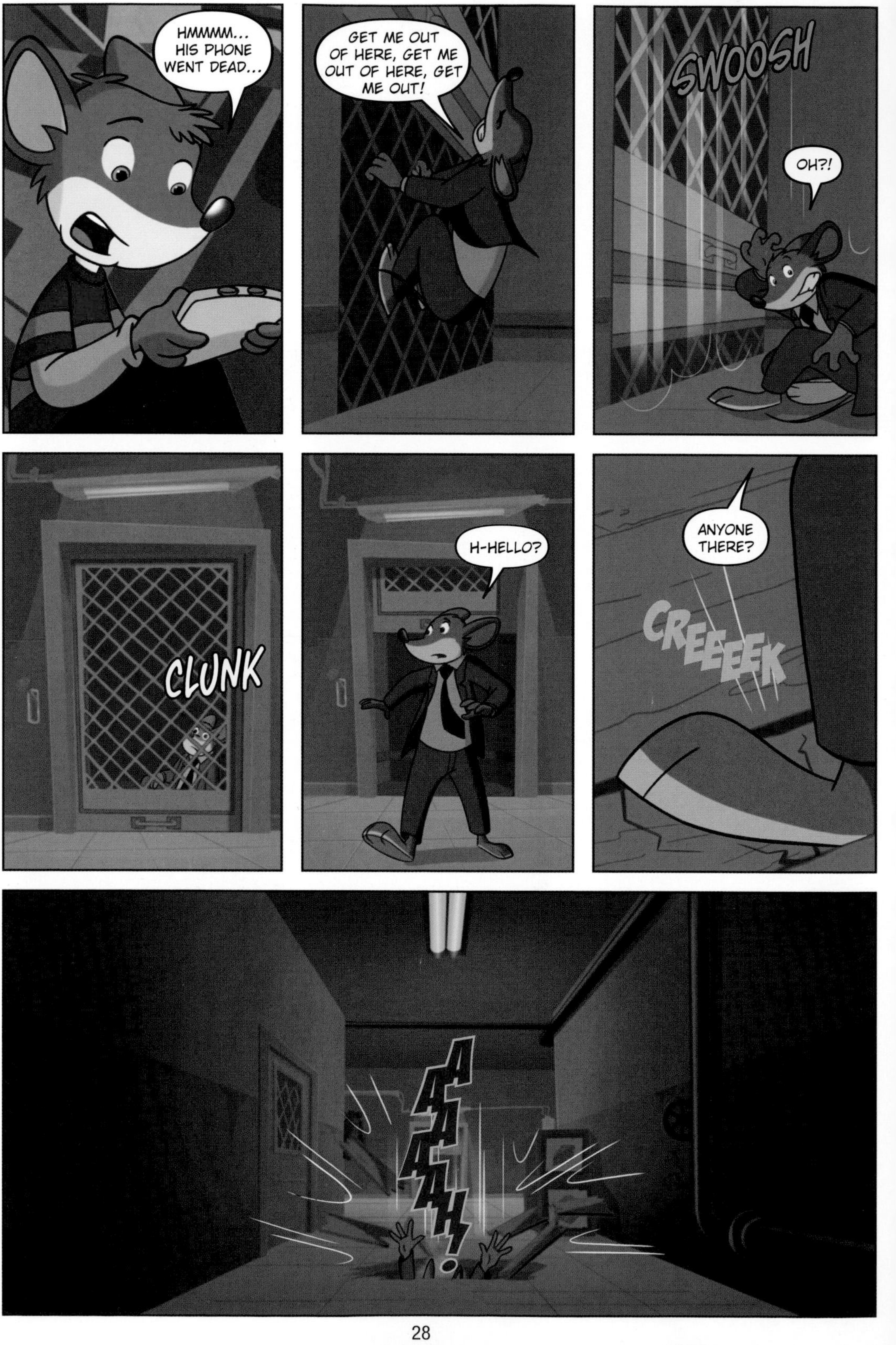
HMMMM... HIS PHONE WENT DEAD...
GET ME OUT OF HERE, GET ME OUT OF HERE, GET ME OUT!
SWOOSH
OH?!
CLUNK
H-HELLO?
ANYONE THERE?
CREEEEK
AAAAAH!

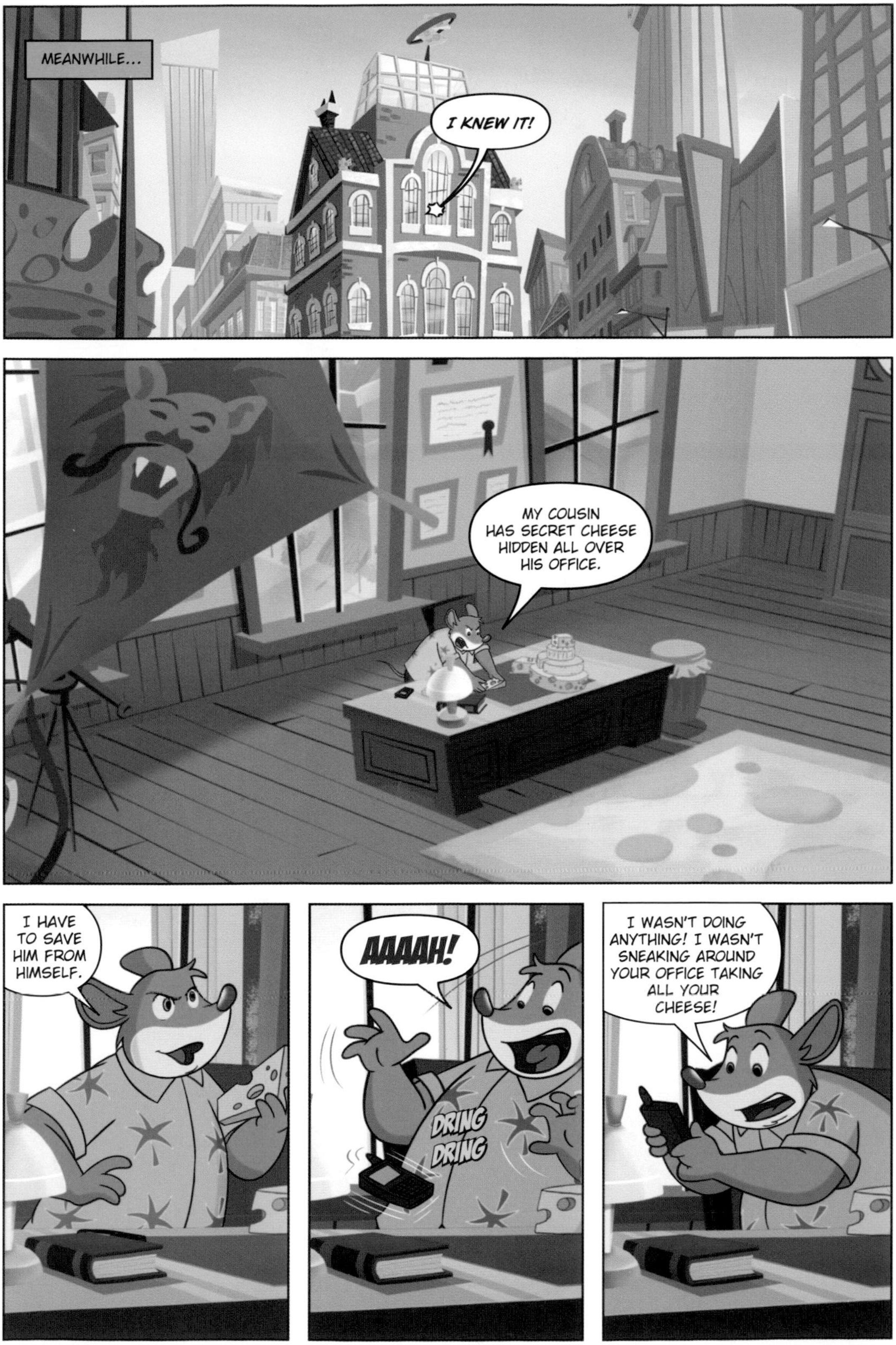
MEANWHILE...
I KNEW IT!
MY COUSIN HAS SECRET CHEESE HIDDEN ALL OVER HIS OFFICE.
I HAVE TO SAVE HIM FROM HIMSELF.
AAAAH!
DRING DRING
I WASN'T DOING ANYTHING! I WASN'T SNEAKING AROUND YOUR OFFICE TAKING ALL YOUR CHEESE!

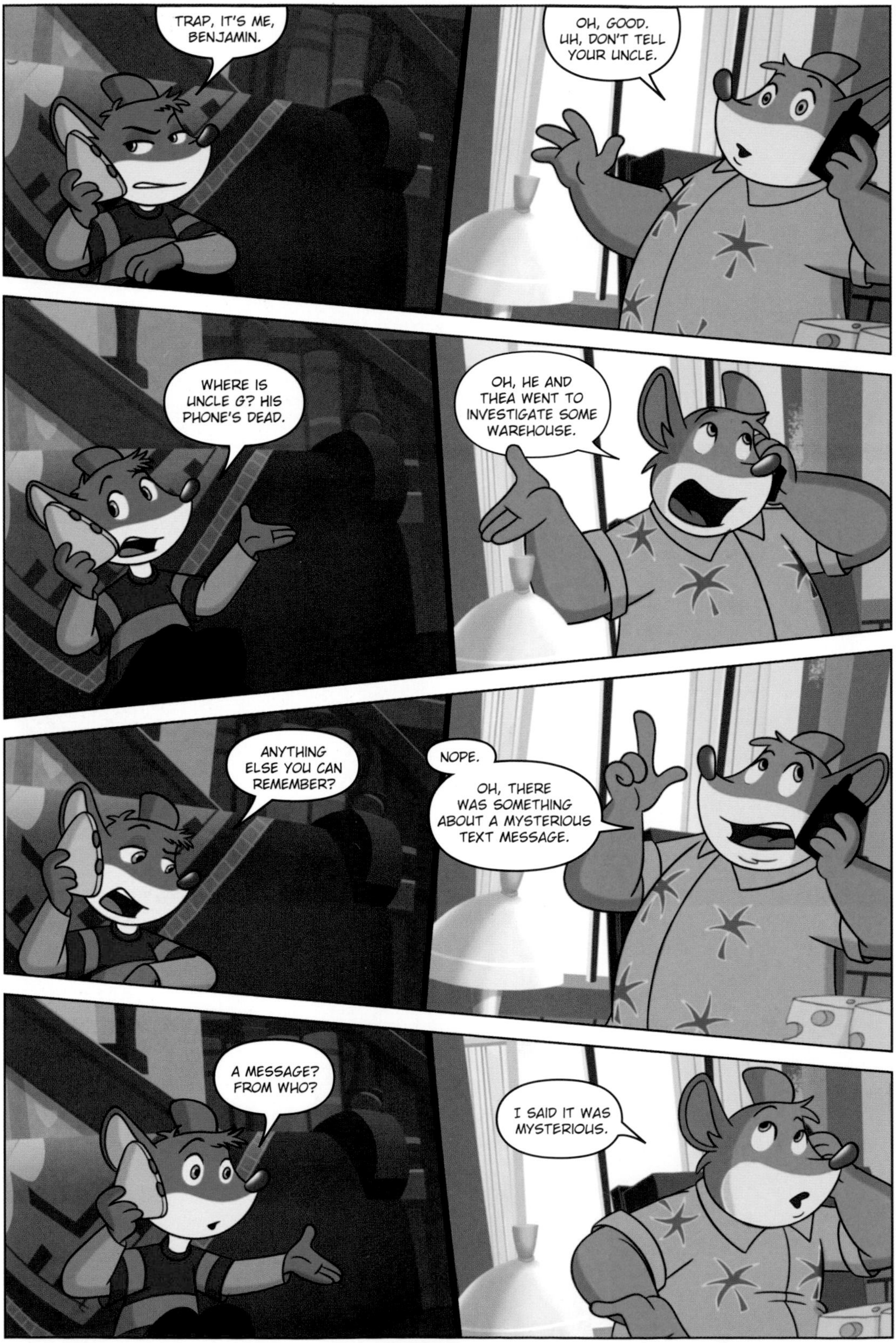
TRAP, IT'S ME, BENJAMIN.
OH, GOOD. UH, DON'T TELL YOUR UNCLE.
WHERE IS UNCLE G? HIS PHONE'S DEAD.
OH, HE AND THEA WENT TO INVESTIGATE SOME WAREHOUSE.
ANYTHING ELSE YOU CAN REMEMBER?
NOPE.
OH, THERE WAS SOMETHING ABOUT A MYSTERIOUS TEXT MESSAGE.
A MESSAGE? FROM WHO?
I SAID IT WAS MYSTERIOUS.

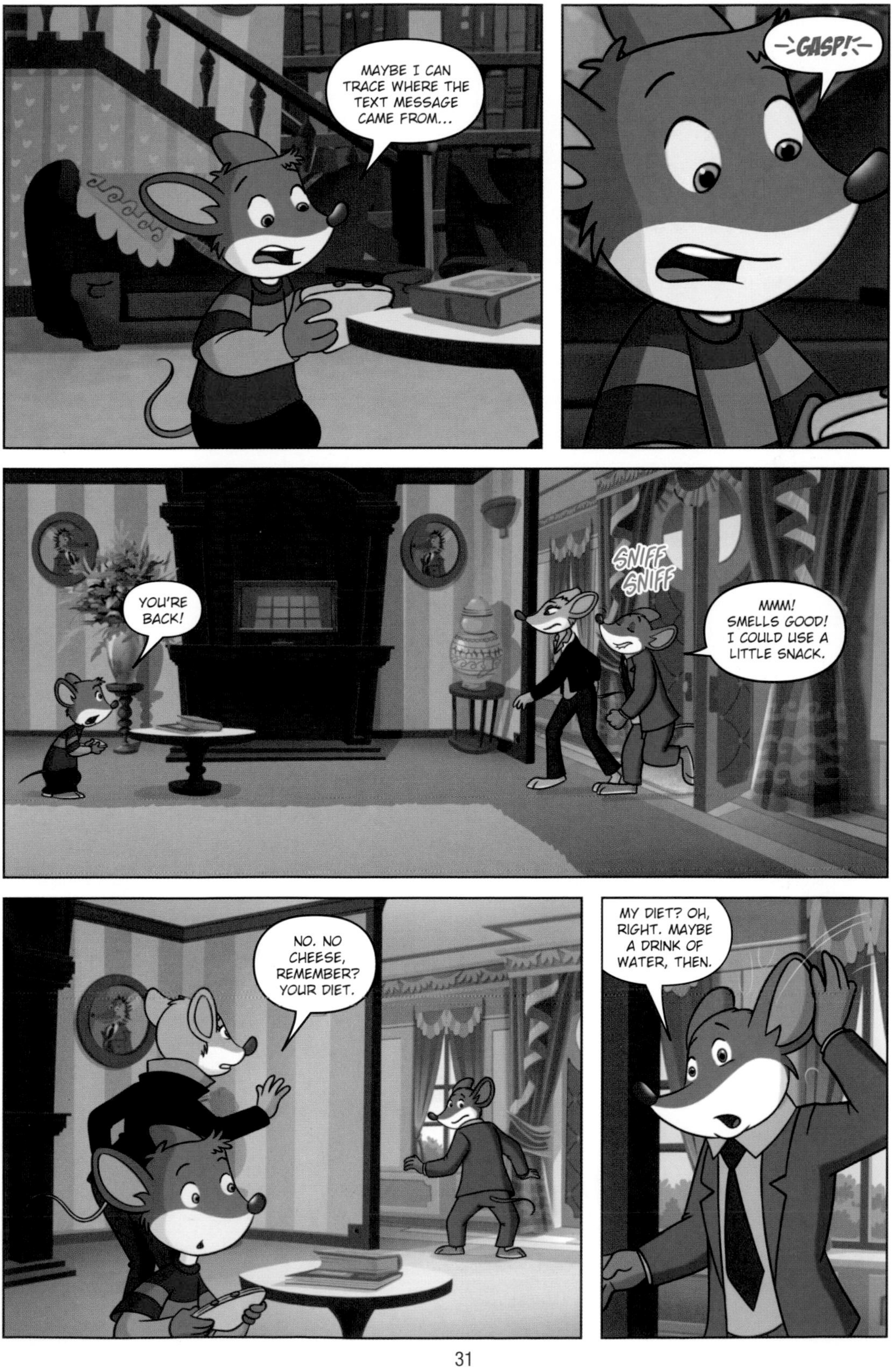
MAYBE I CAN TRACE WHERE THE TEXT MESSAGE CAME FROM...
-GASP!-
YOU'RE BACK!
SNIFF SNIFF
MMM! SMELLS GOOD! I COULD USE A LITTLE SNACK.
NO. NO CHEESE, REMEMBER? YOUR DIET.
MY DIET? OH, RIGHT. MAYBE A DRINK OF WATER, THEN.

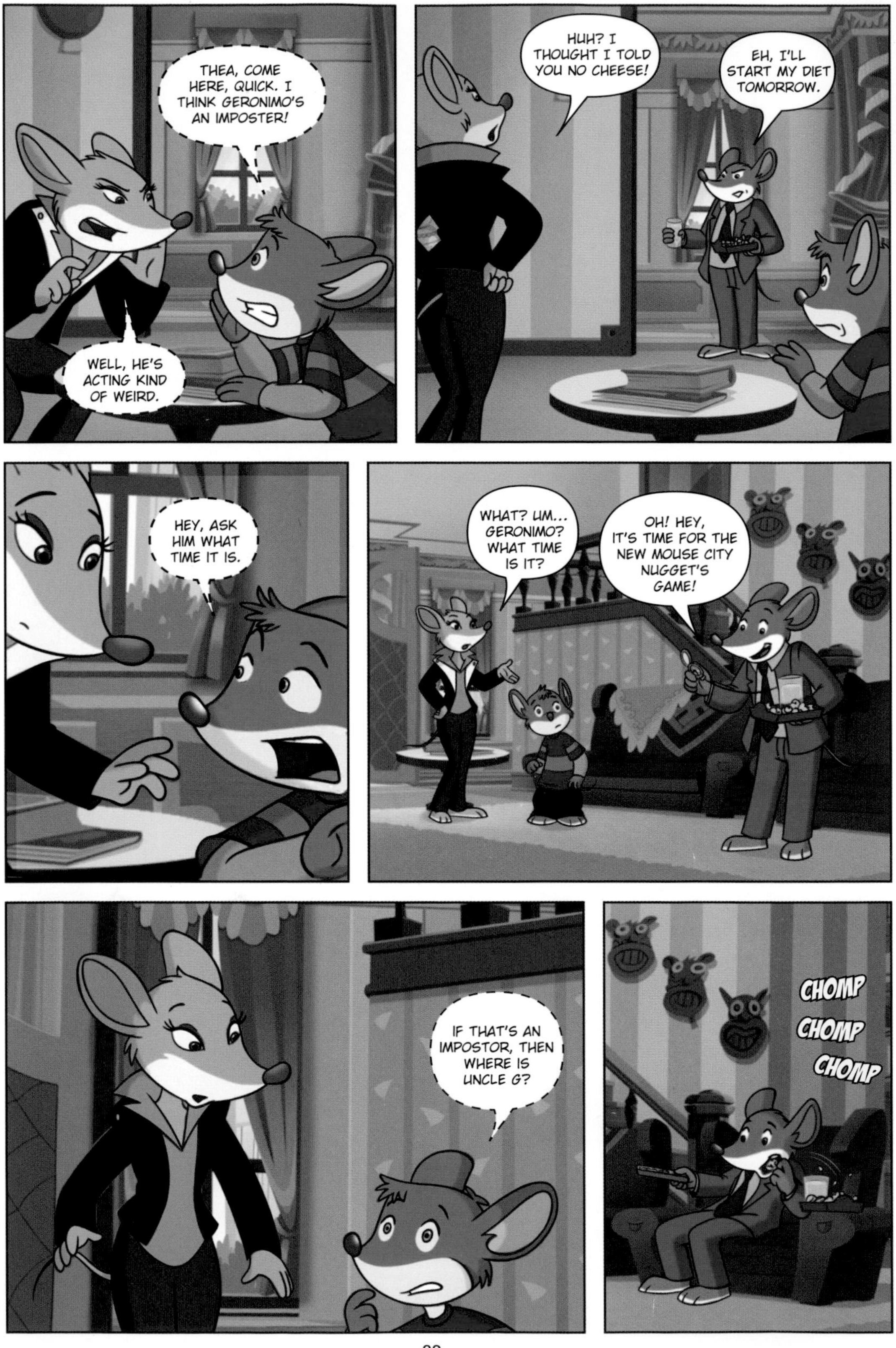
THEA, COME HERE, QUICK. I THINK GERONIMO'S AN IMPOSTER!
WELL, HE'S ACTING KIND OF WEIRD.
HUH? I THOUGHT I TOLD YOU NO CHEESE!
EH, I'LL START MY DIET TOMORROW.
HEY, ASK HIM WHAT TIME IT IS.
WHAT? UM... GERONIMO? WHAT TIME IS IT?
OH! HEY, IT'S TIME FOR THE NEW MOUSE CITY NUGGET'S GAME!
IF THAT'S AN IMPOSTOR, THEN WHERE IS UNCLE G?
CHOMP
CHOMP
CHOMP

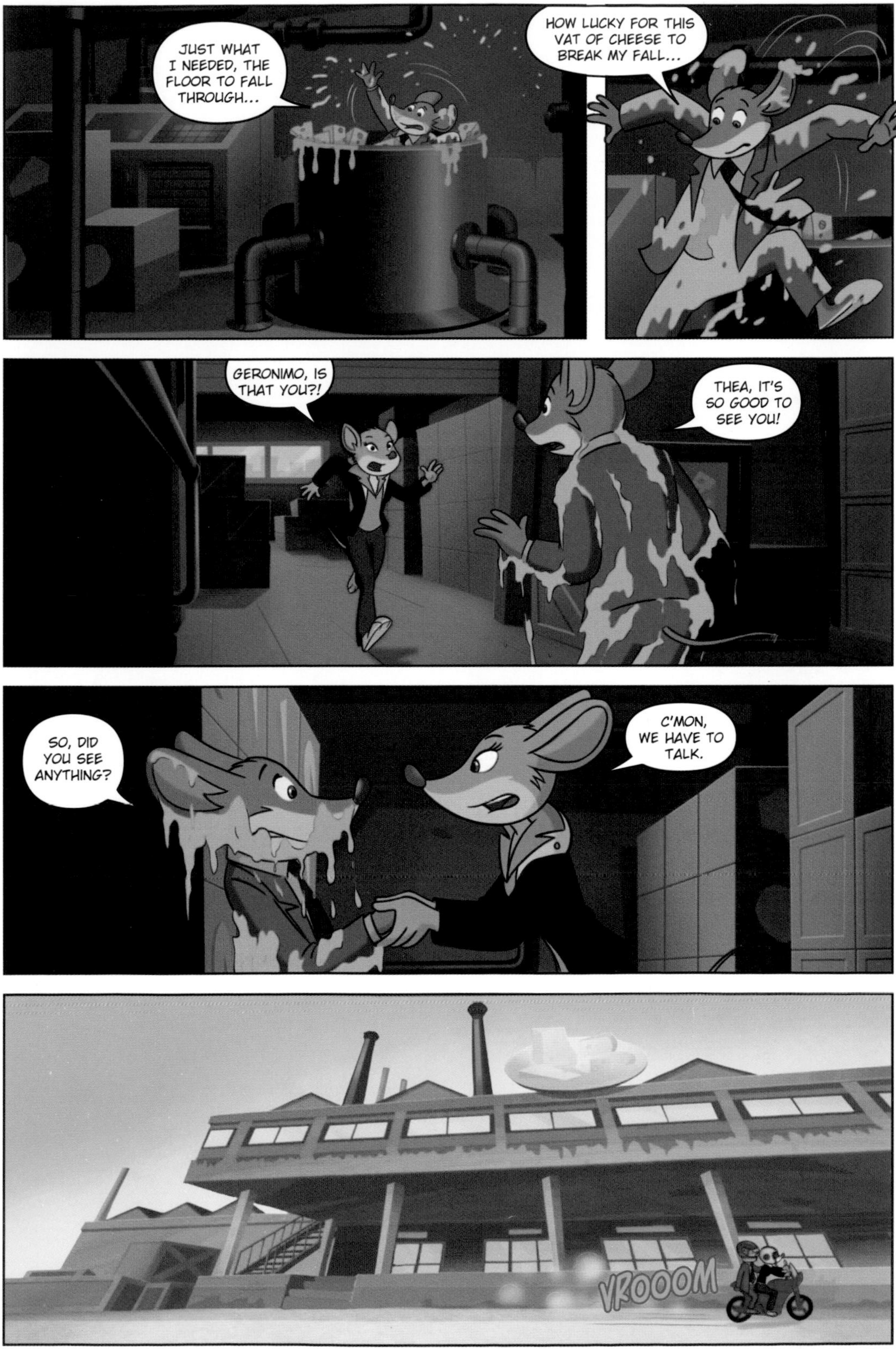
JUST WHAT I NEEDED, THE FLOOR TO FALL THROUGH...
HOW LUCKY FOR THIS VAT OF CHEESE TO BREAK MY FALL...
GERONIMO, IS THAT YOU?!
THEA, IT'S SO GOOD TO SEE YOU!
SO, DID YOU SEE ANYTHING?
C'MON, WE HAVE TO TALK.
VROOOM

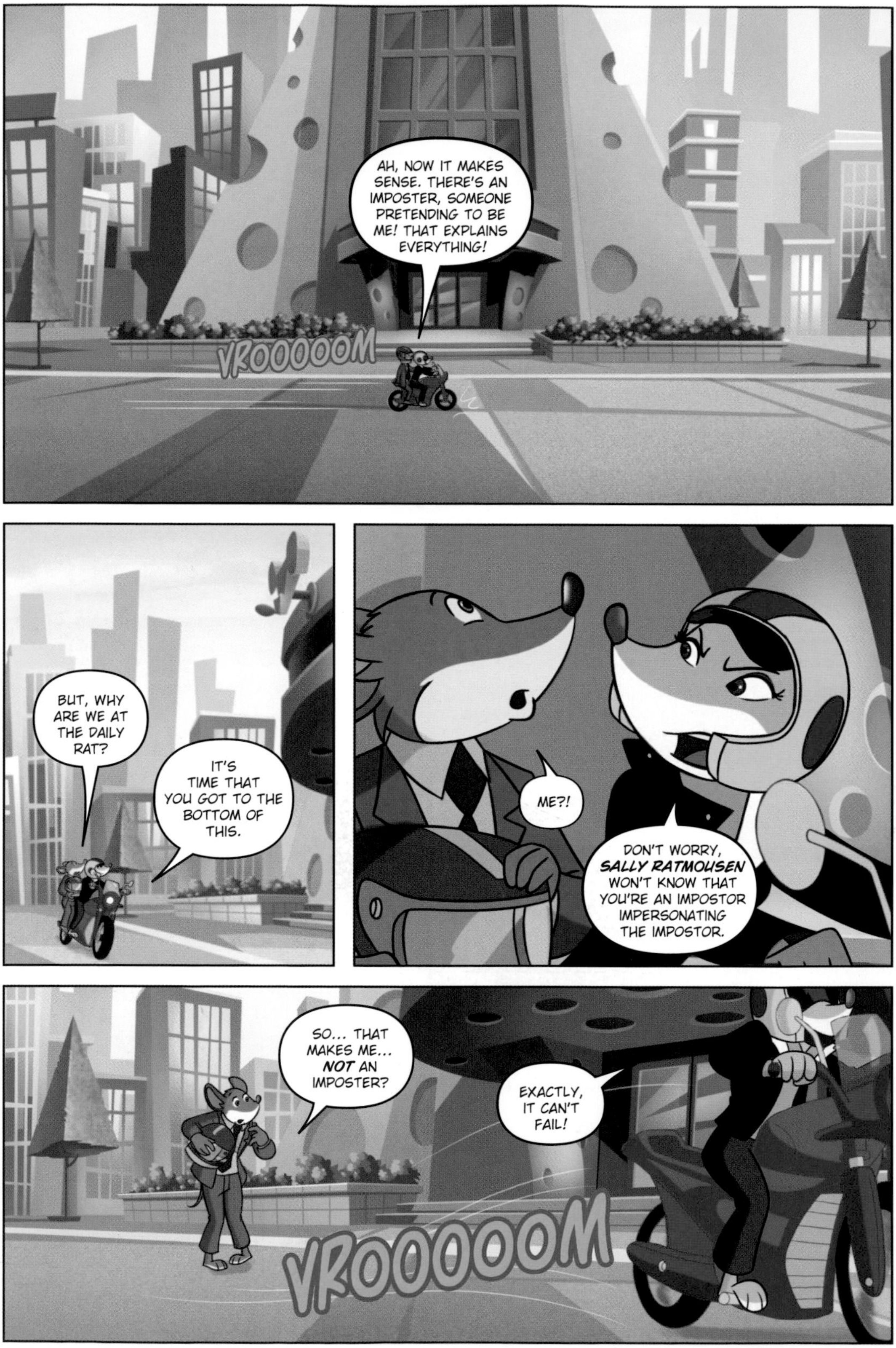
AH, NOW IT MAKES SENSE. THERE'S AN IMPOSTER, SOMEONE PRETENDING TO BE ME! THAT EXPLAINS EVERYTHING!
VROOOOOM
BUT, WHY ARE WE AT THE DAILY RAT?
IT'S TIME THAT YOU GOT TO THE BOTTOM OF THIS.
ME?!
DON'T WORRY, **SALLY RATMOUSEN** WON'T KNOW THAT YOU'RE AN IMPOSTOR IMPERSONATING THE IMPOSTOR.
SO... THAT MAKES ME... ***NOT*** AN IMPOSTER?
EXACTLY, IT CAN'T FAIL!
VROOOOOM

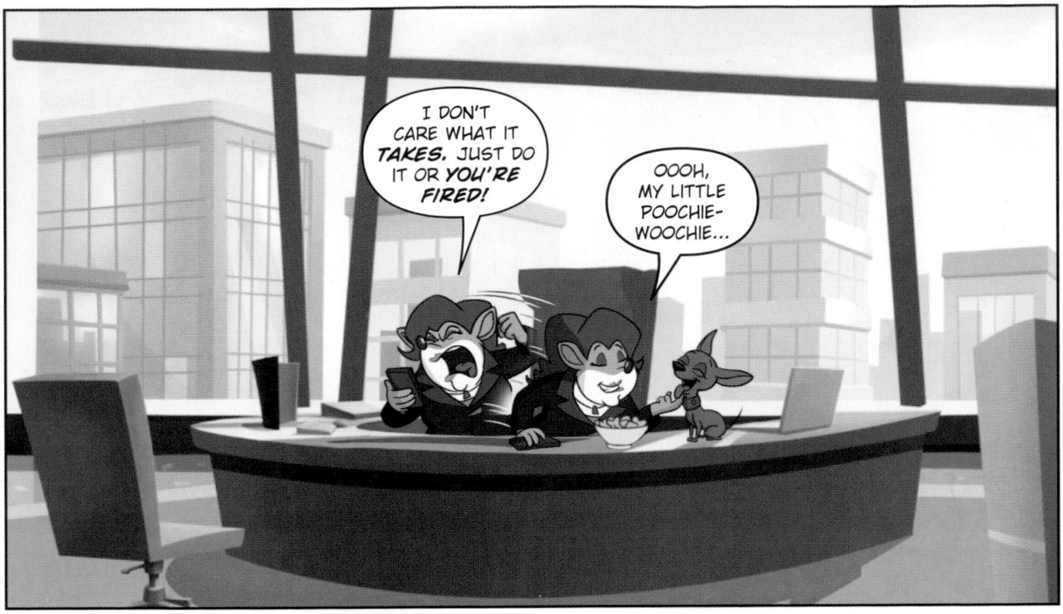
I DON'T CARE WHAT IT *TAKES.* JUST DO IT OR *YOU'RE FIRED!*
OOOH, MY LITTLE POOCHIE-WOOCHIE...

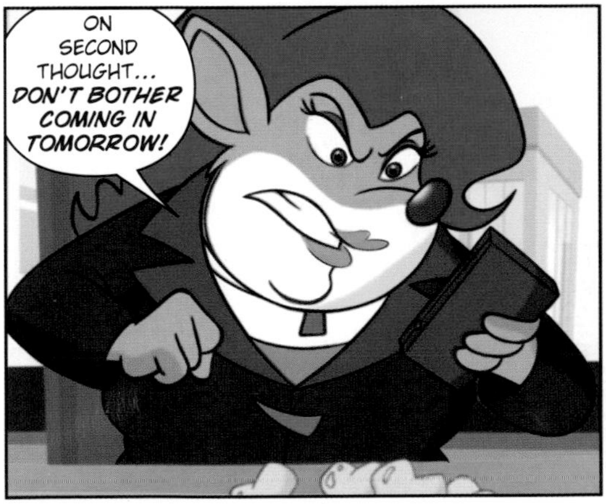
ON SECOND THOUGHT... *DON'T BOTHER COMING IN TOMORROW!*

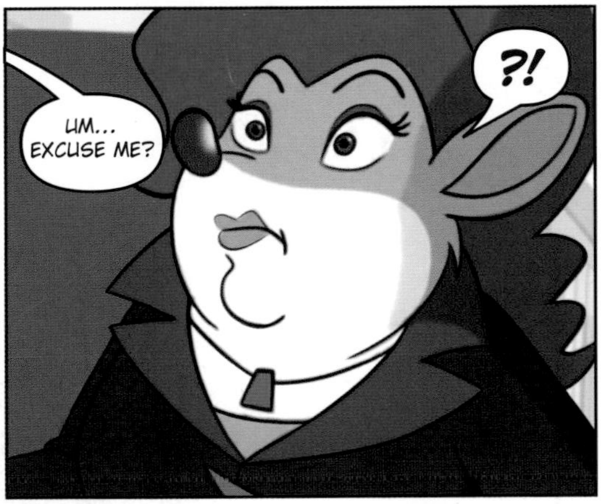
UM... EXCUSE ME?
?!

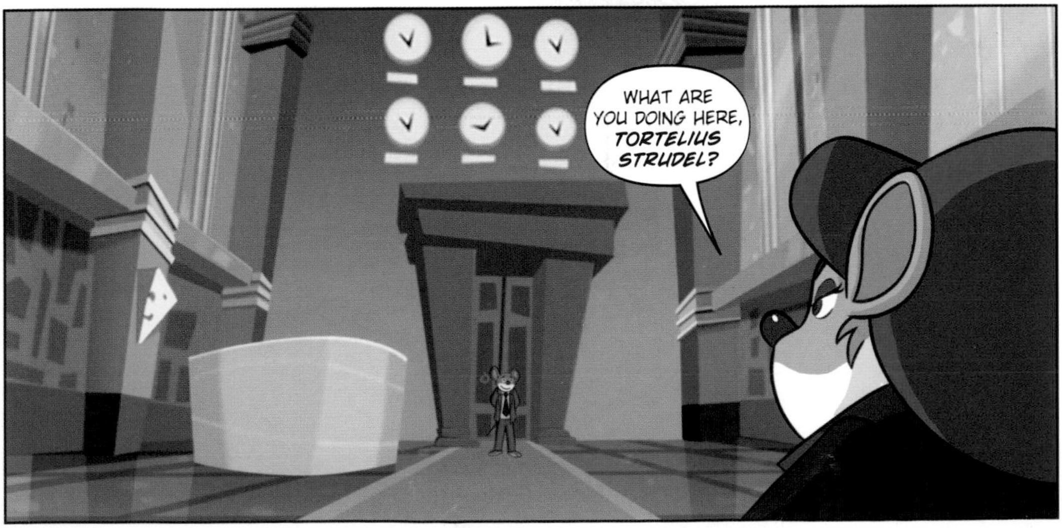
WHAT ARE YOU DOING HERE, *TORTELIUS STRUDEL?*

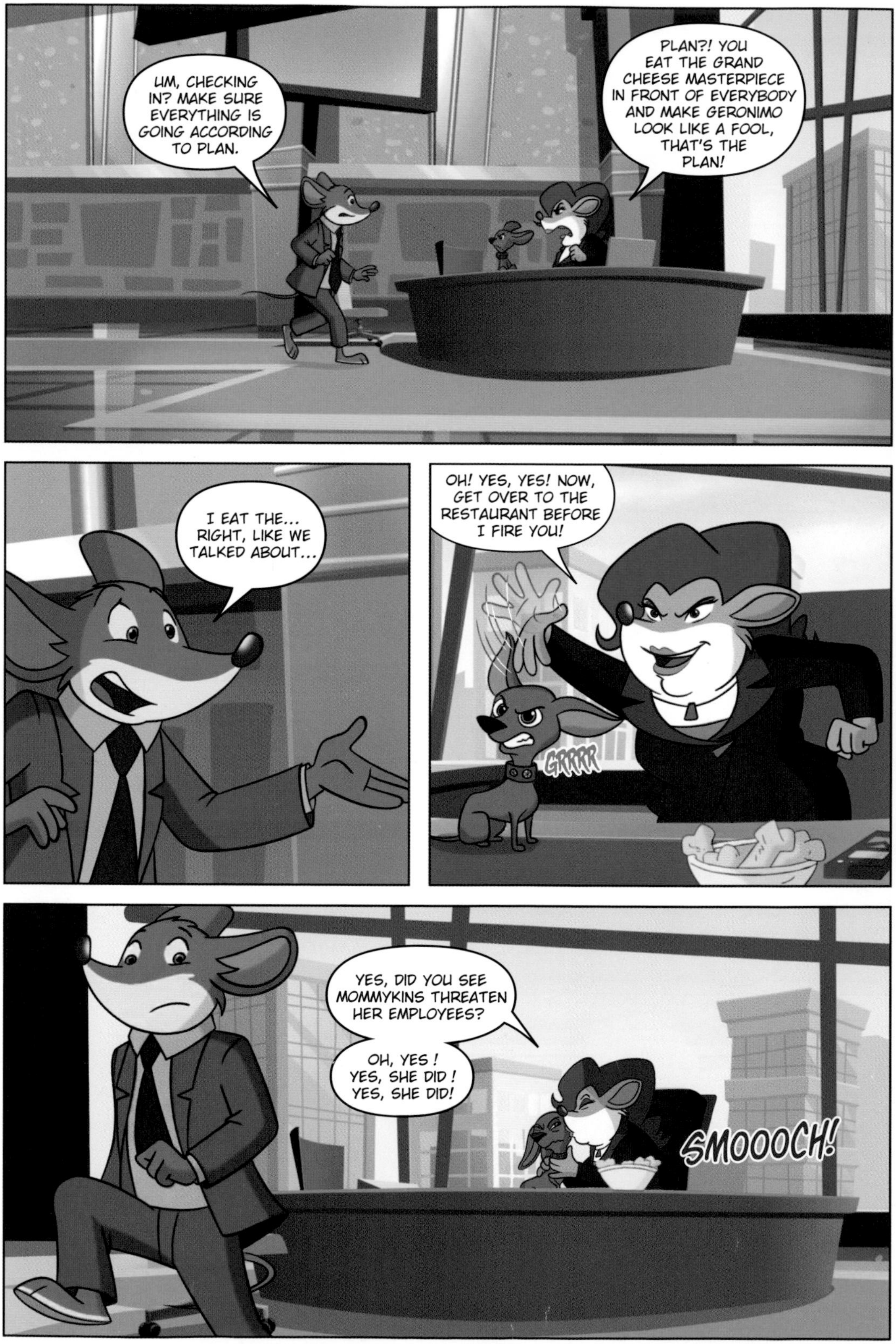
UM, CHECKING IN? MAKE SURE EVERYTHING IS GOING ACCORDING TO PLAN.
PLAN?! YOU EAT THE GRAND CHEESE MASTERPIECE IN FRONT OF EVERYBODY AND MAKE GERONIMO LOOK LIKE A FOOL, THAT'S THE PLAN!
I EAT THE... RIGHT, LIKE WE TALKED ABOUT...
OH! YES, YES! NOW, GET OVER TO THE RESTAURANT BEFORE I FIRE YOU!
GRRRR
YES, DID YOU SEE MOMMYKINS THREATEN HER EMPLOYEES?
OH, YES ! YES, SHE DID ! YES, SHE DID!
SMOOOCH!

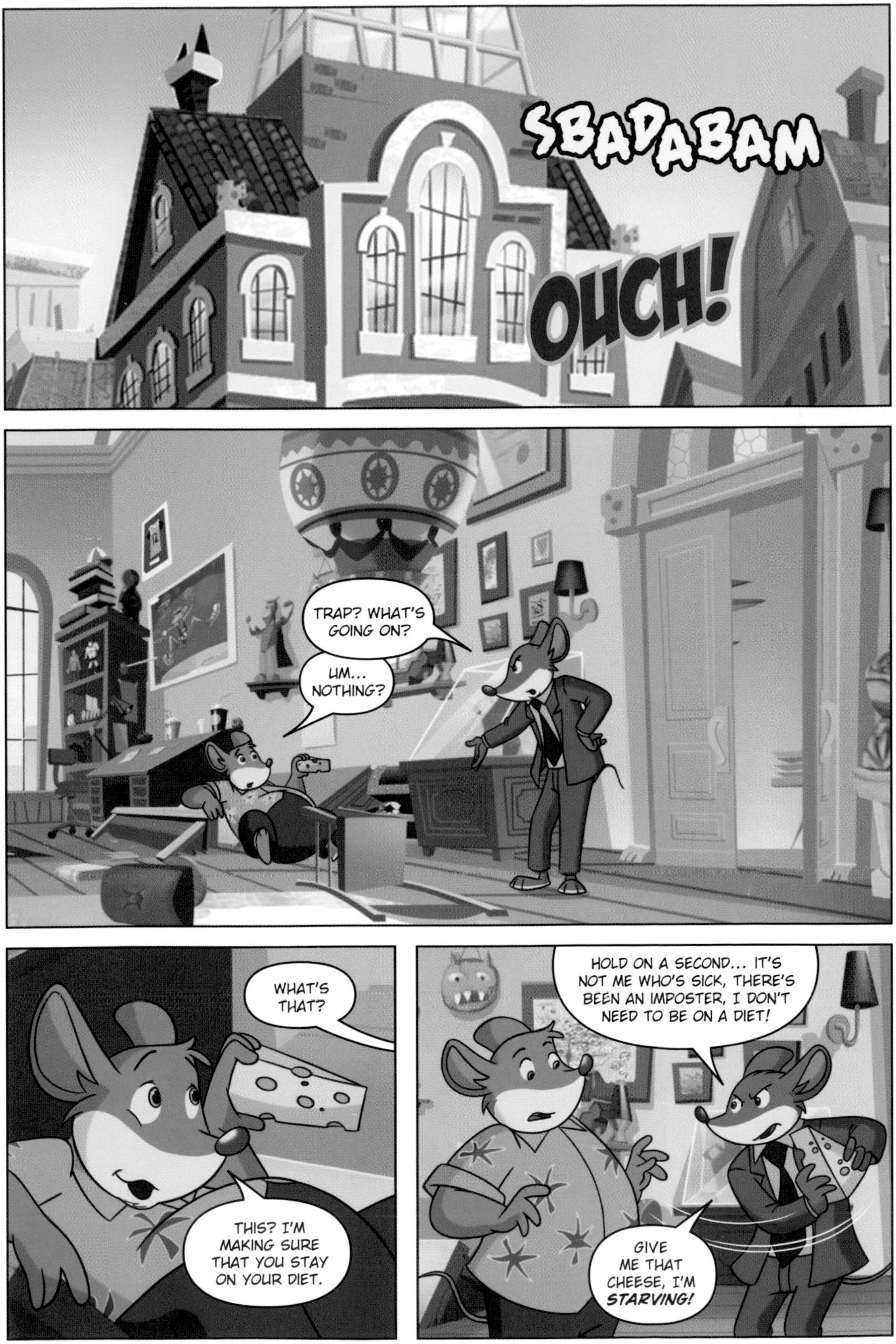
SBADABAM
OUCH!
TRAP? WHAT'S GOING ON?
UM... NOTHING?
WHAT'S THAT?
THIS? I'M MAKING SURE THAT YOU STAY ON YOUR DIET.
HOLD ON A SECOND... IT'S NOT ME WHO'S SICK, THERE'S BEEN AN IMPOSTER, I DON'T NEED TO BE ON A DIET!
GIVE ME THAT CHEESE, I'M **STARVING!**

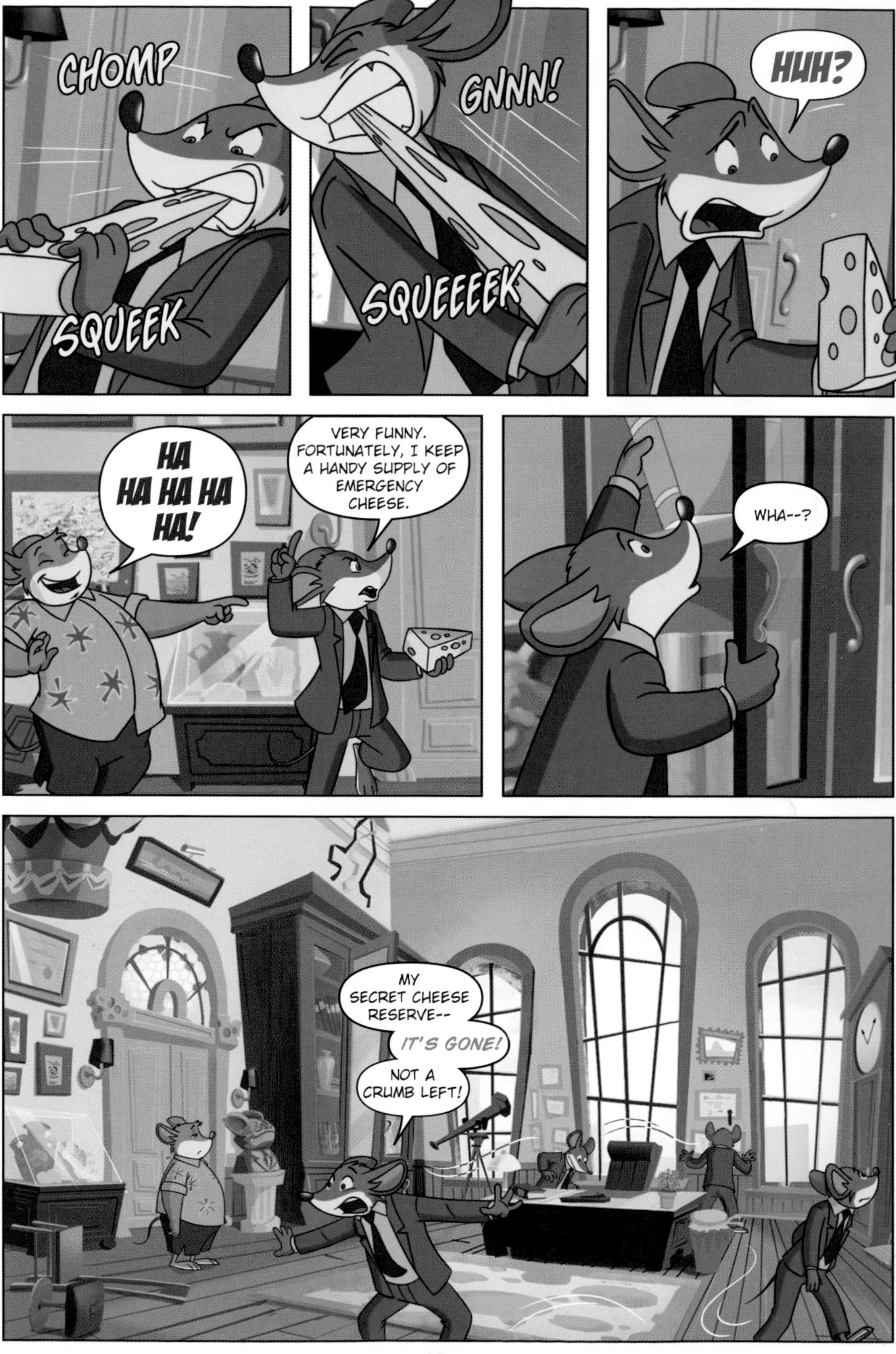
CHOMP
SQUEEK
GNNN!
SQUEEEEK
HUH?
HA HA HA HA HA!
VERY FUNNY. FORTUNATELY, I KEEP A HANDY SUPPLY OF EMERGENCY CHEESE.
WHA--?
MY SECRET CHEESE RESERVE--
IT'S GONE!
NOT A CRUMB LEFT!

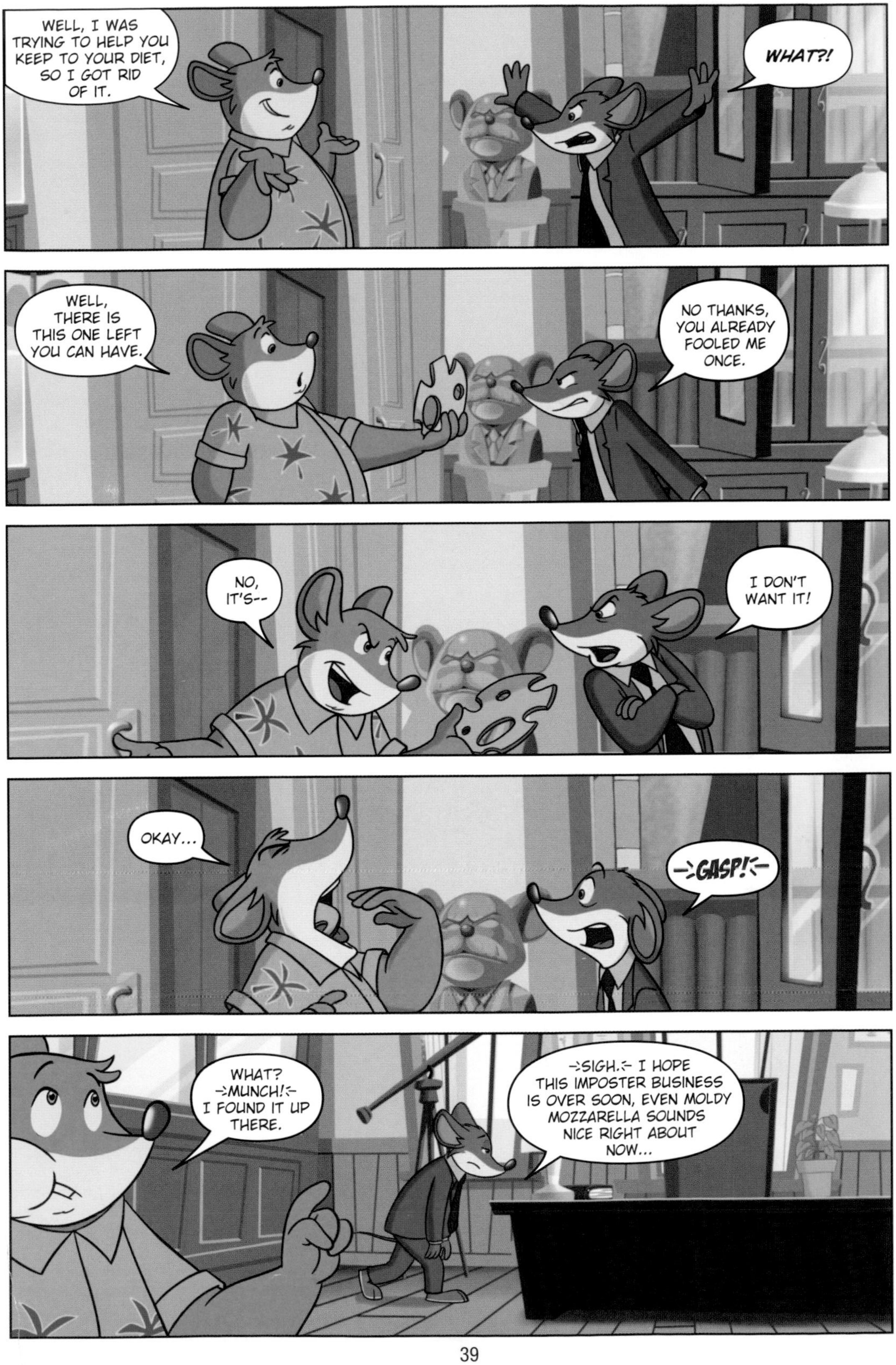
WELL, I WAS TRYING TO HELP YOU KEEP TO YOUR DIET, SO I GOT RID OF IT.
WHAT?!
WELL, THERE IS THIS ONE LEFT YOU CAN HAVE.
NO THANKS, YOU ALREADY FOOLED ME ONCE.
NO, IT'S--
I DON'T WANT IT!
OKAY...
-GASP!-
WHAT? -MUNCH!- I FOUND IT UP THERE.
-SIGH.- I HOPE THIS IMPOSTER BUSINESS IS OVER SOON, EVEN MOLDY MOZZARELLA SOUNDS NICE RIGHT ABOUT NOW...

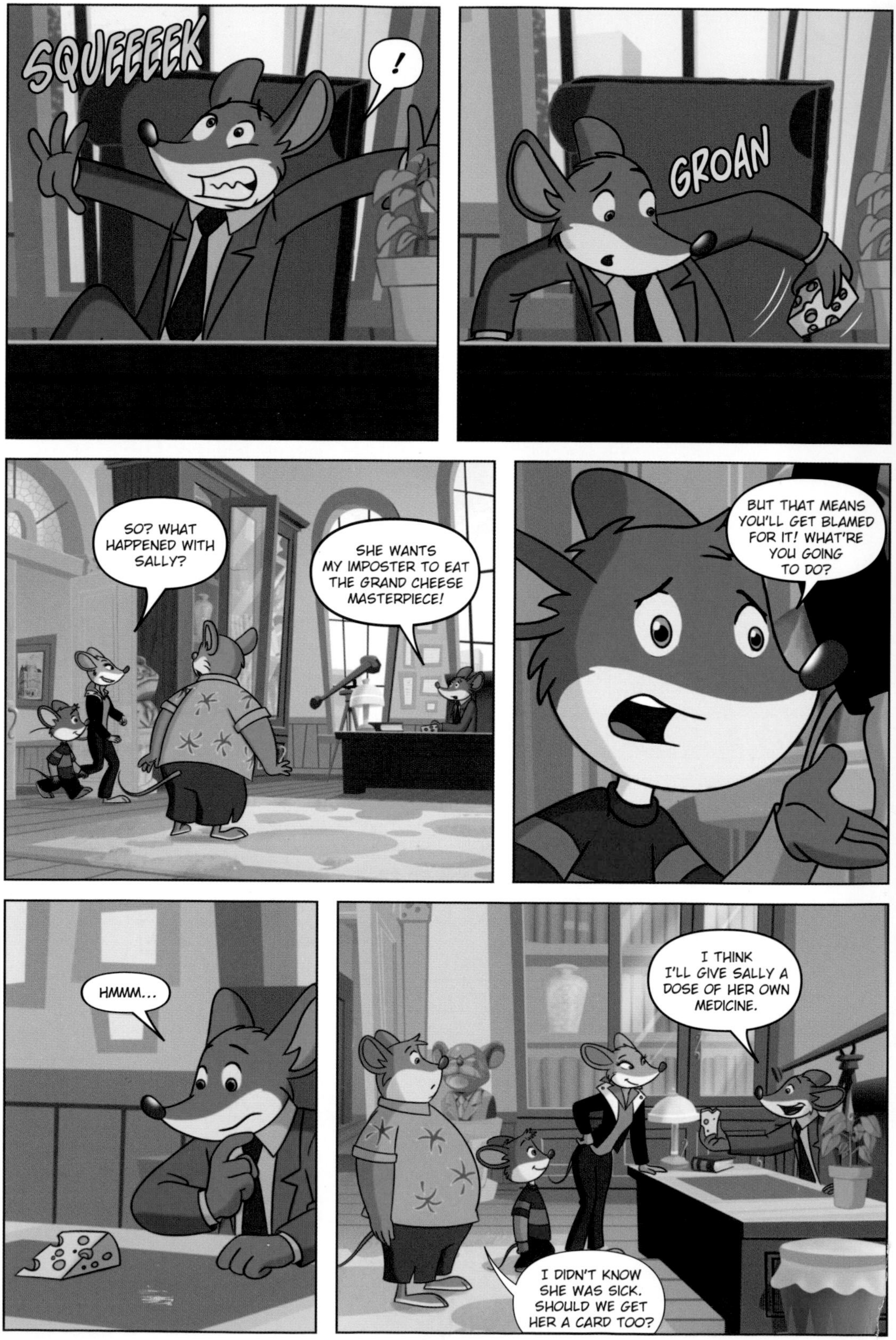
SQUEEEEK
!
GROAN
SO? WHAT HAPPENED WITH SALLY?
SHE WANTS MY IMPOSTER TO EAT THE GRAND CHEESE MASTERPIECE!
BUT THAT MEANS YOU'LL GET BLAMED FOR IT! WHAT'RE YOU GOING TO DO?
HMMM...
I THINK I'LL GIVE SALLY A DOSE OF HER OWN MEDICINE.
I DIDN'T KNOW SHE WAS SICK. SHOULD WE GET HER A CARD TOO?

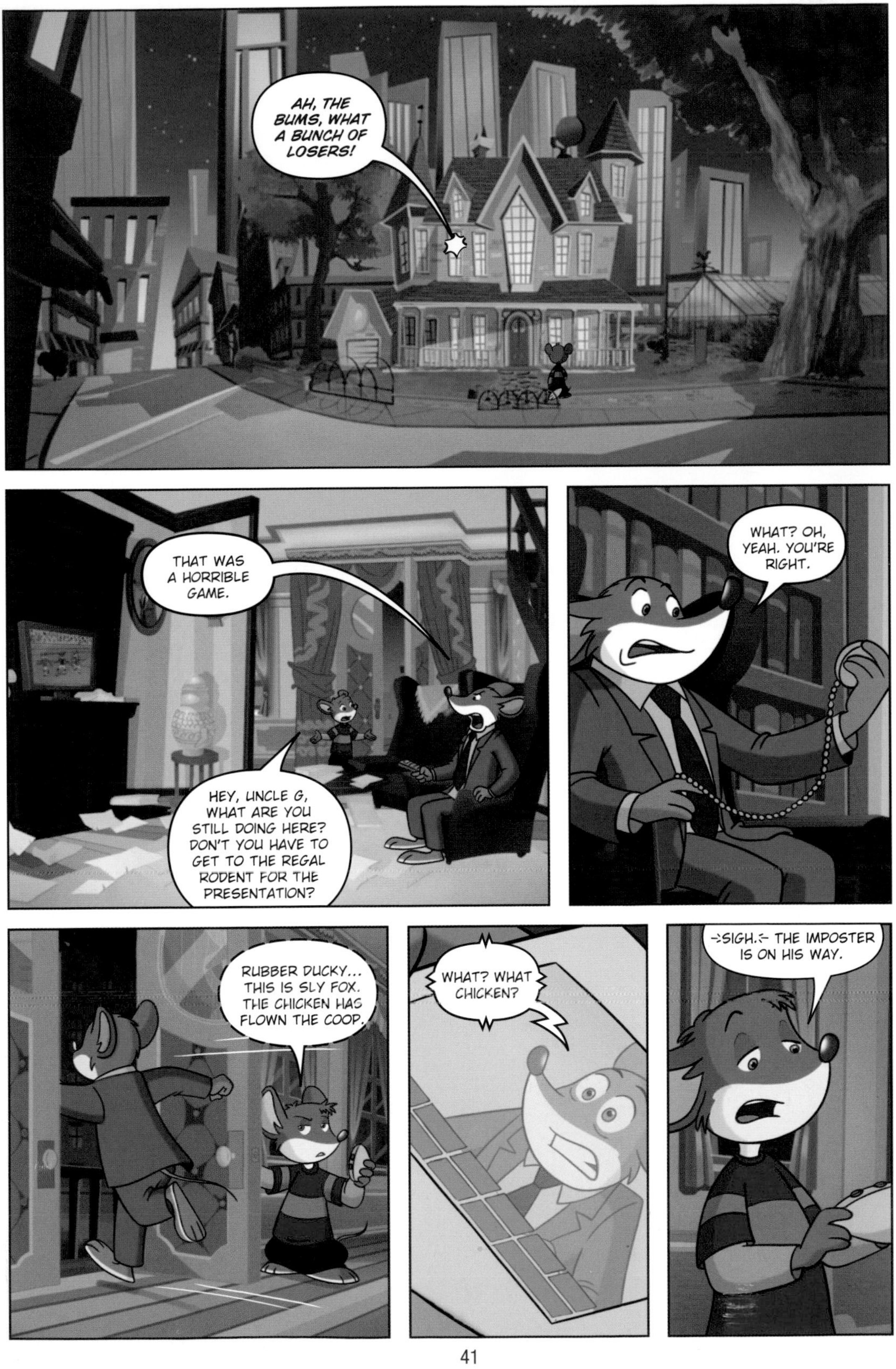
AH, THE BUMS, WHAT A BUNCH OF LOSERS!
THAT WAS A HORRIBLE GAME.
HEY, UNCLE G, WHAT ARE YOU STILL DOING HERE? DON'T YOU HAVE TO GET TO THE REGAL RODENT FOR THE PRESENTATION?
WHAT? OH, YEAH. YOU'RE RIGHT.
RUBBER DUCKY... THIS IS SLY FOX. THE CHICKEN HAS FLOWN THE COOP.
WHAT? WHAT CHICKEN?
SIGH. THE IMPOSTER IS ON HIS WAY.

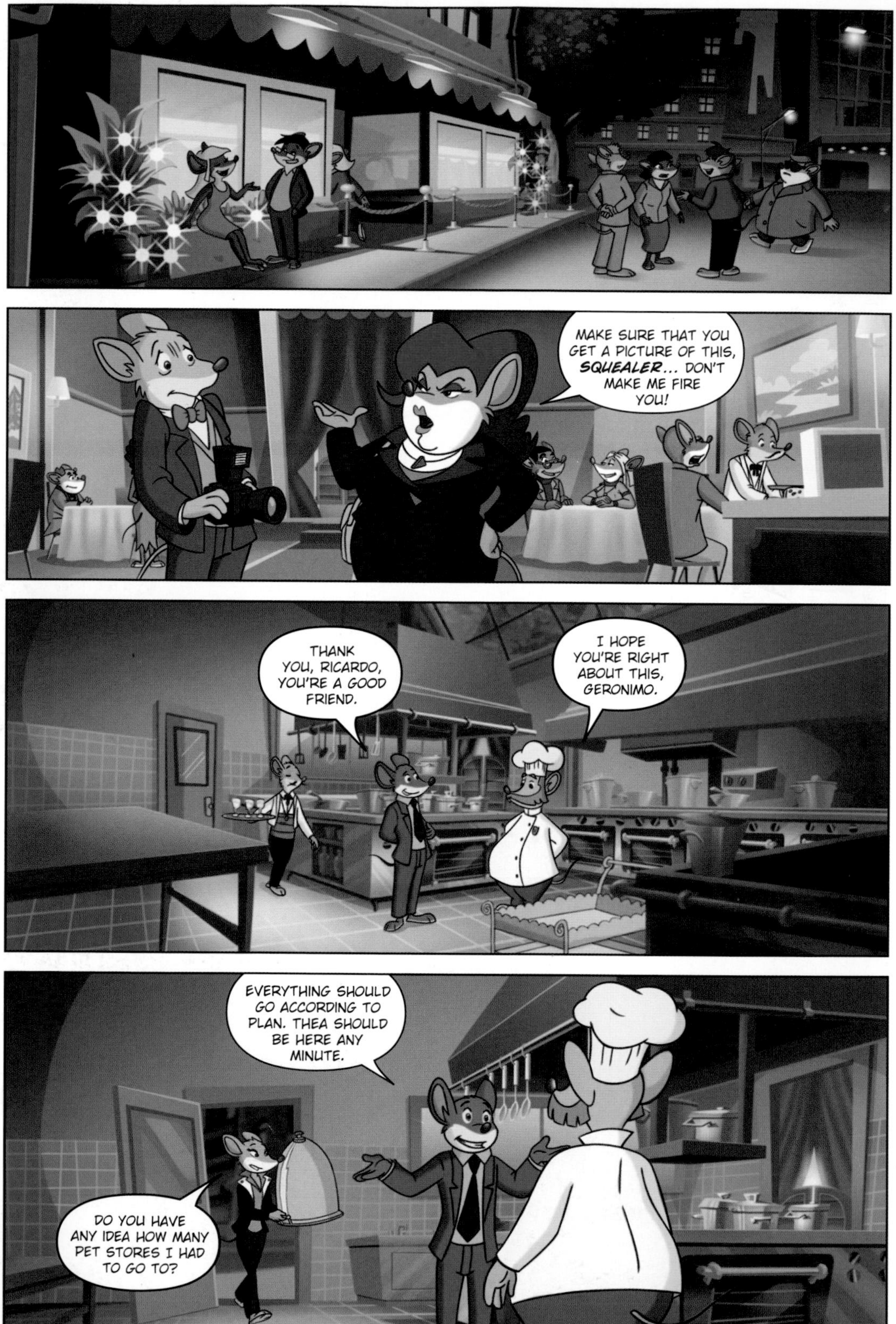
MAKE SURE THAT YOU GET A PICTURE OF THIS, SQUEALER... DON'T MAKE ME FIRE YOU!
THANK YOU, RICARDO, YOU'RE A GOOD FRIEND.
I HOPE YOU'RE RIGHT ABOUT THIS, GERONIMO.
EVERYTHING SHOULD GO ACCORDING TO PLAN. THEA SHOULD BE HERE ANY MINUTE.
DO YOU HAVE ANY IDEA HOW MANY PET STORES I HAD TO GO TO?

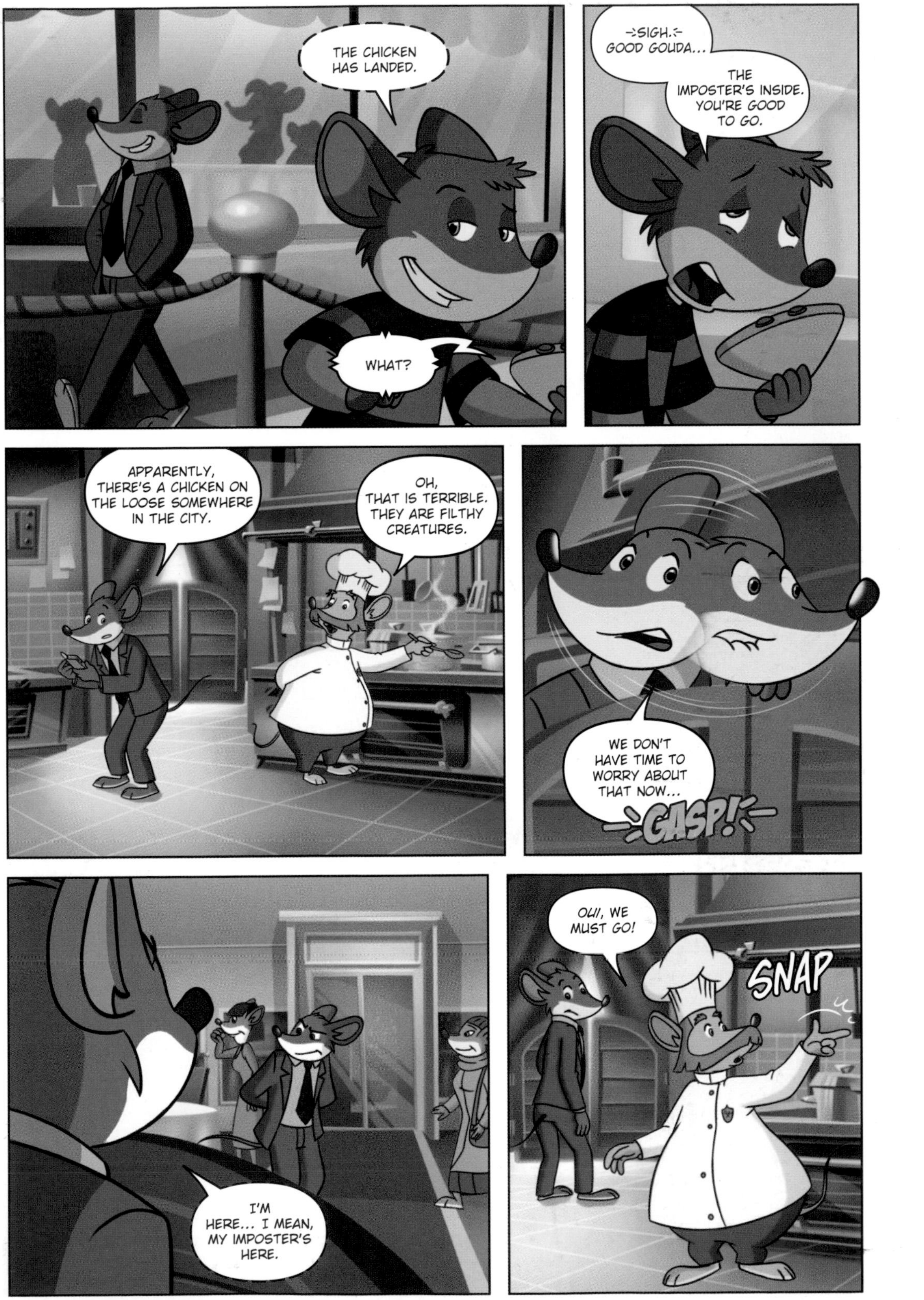
THE CHICKEN HAS LANDED.
WHAT?
-SIGH.- GOOD GOUDA...
THE IMPOSTER'S INSIDE. YOU'RE GOOD TO GO.
APPARENTLY, THERE'S A CHICKEN ON THE LOOSE SOMEWHERE IN THE CITY.
OH, THAT IS TERRIBLE. THEY ARE FILTHY CREATURES.
WE DON'T HAVE TIME TO WORRY ABOUT THAT NOW...
GASP!
I'M HERE... I MEAN, MY IMPOSTER'S HERE.
OUI, WE MUST GO!
SNAP

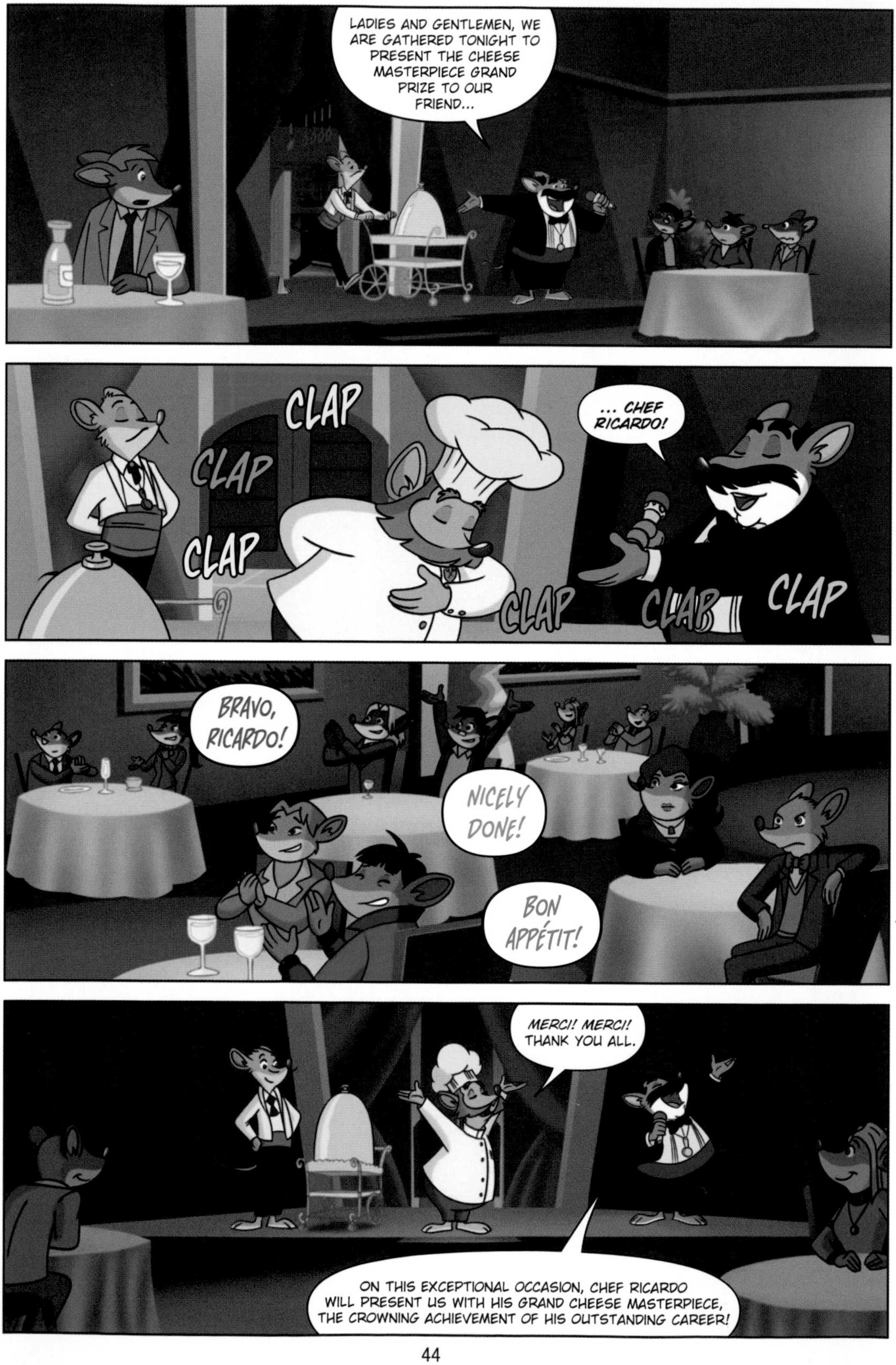
LADIES AND GENTLEMEN, WE ARE GATHERED TONIGHT TO PRESENT THE CHEESE MASTERPIECE GRAND PRIZE TO OUR FRIEND...
CLAP
CLAP
CLAP
... CHEF RICARDO!
CLAP
CLAP
CLAP
BRAVO, RICARDO!
NICELY DONE!
BON APPÉTIT!
MERCI! MERCI! THANK YOU ALL.
ON THIS EXCEPTIONAL OCCASION, CHEF RICARDO WILL PRESENT US WITH HIS GRAND CHEESE MASTERPIECE, THE CROWNING ACHIEVEMENT OF HIS OUTSTANDING CAREER!

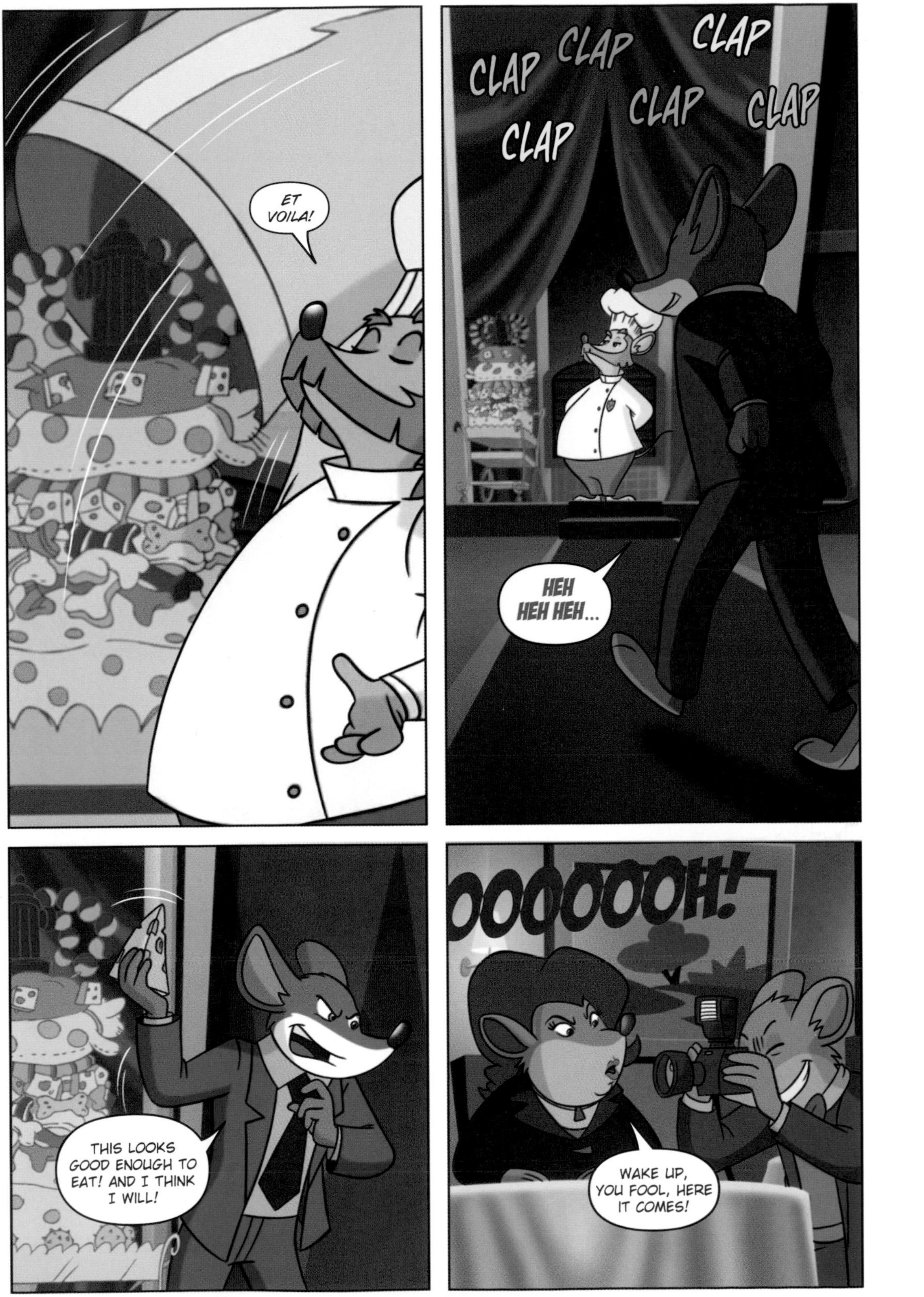
ET VOILA!
CLAP CLAP CLAP CLAP CLAP CLAP
HEH HEH HEH...
THIS LOOKS GOOD ENOUGH TO EAT! AND I THINK I WILL!
OOOOOOOH!
WAKE UP, YOU FOOL, HERE IT COMES!

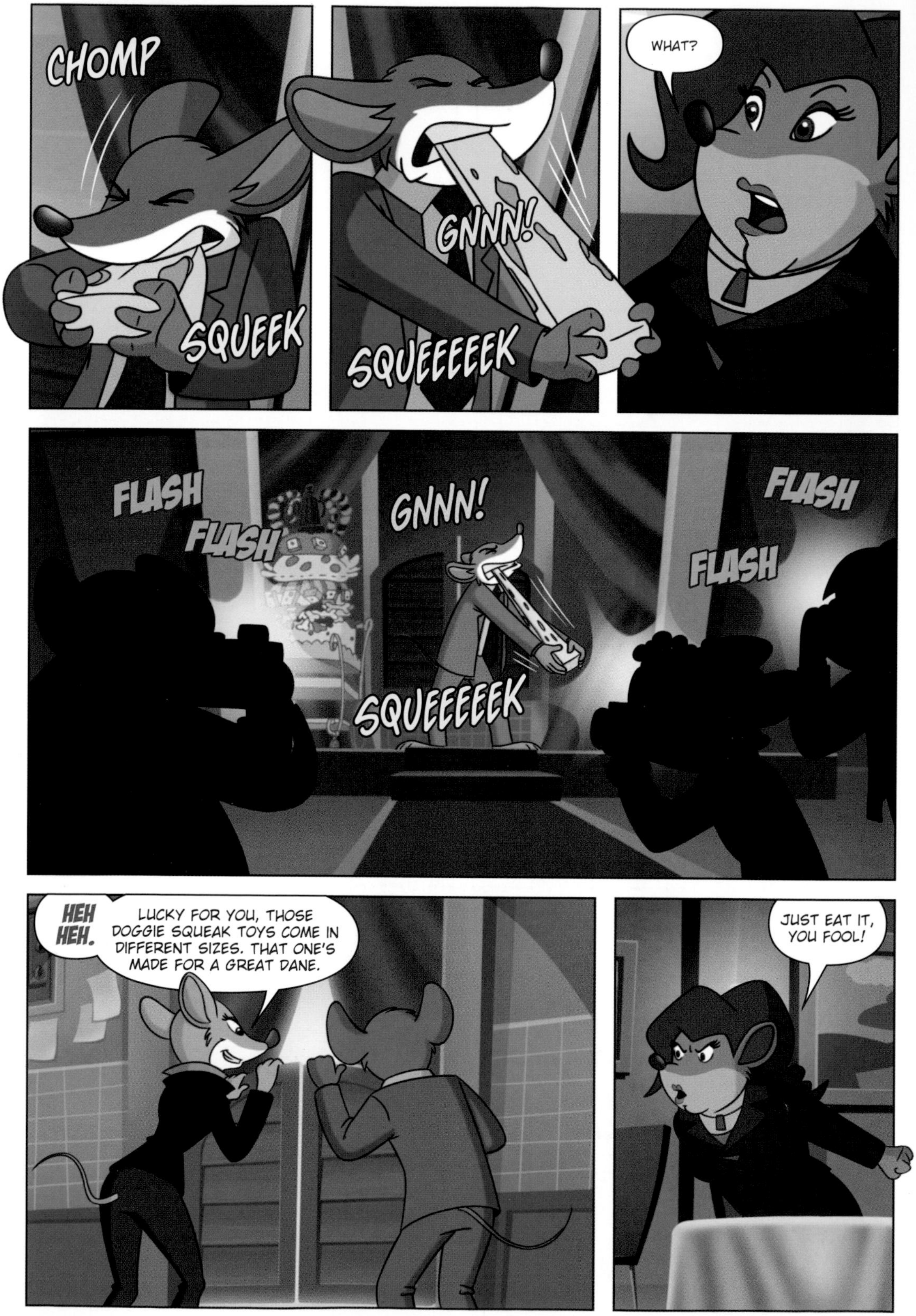
CHOMP
SQUEEK
GNNN!
SQUEEEEEK
WHAT?
FLASH
FLASH
GNNN!
FLASH
FLASH
SQUEEEEEK
HEH HEH.
LUCKY FOR YOU, THOSE DOGGIE SQUEAK TOYS COME IN DIFFERENT SIZES. THAT ONE'S MADE FOR A GREAT DANE.
JUST EAT IT, YOU FOOL!

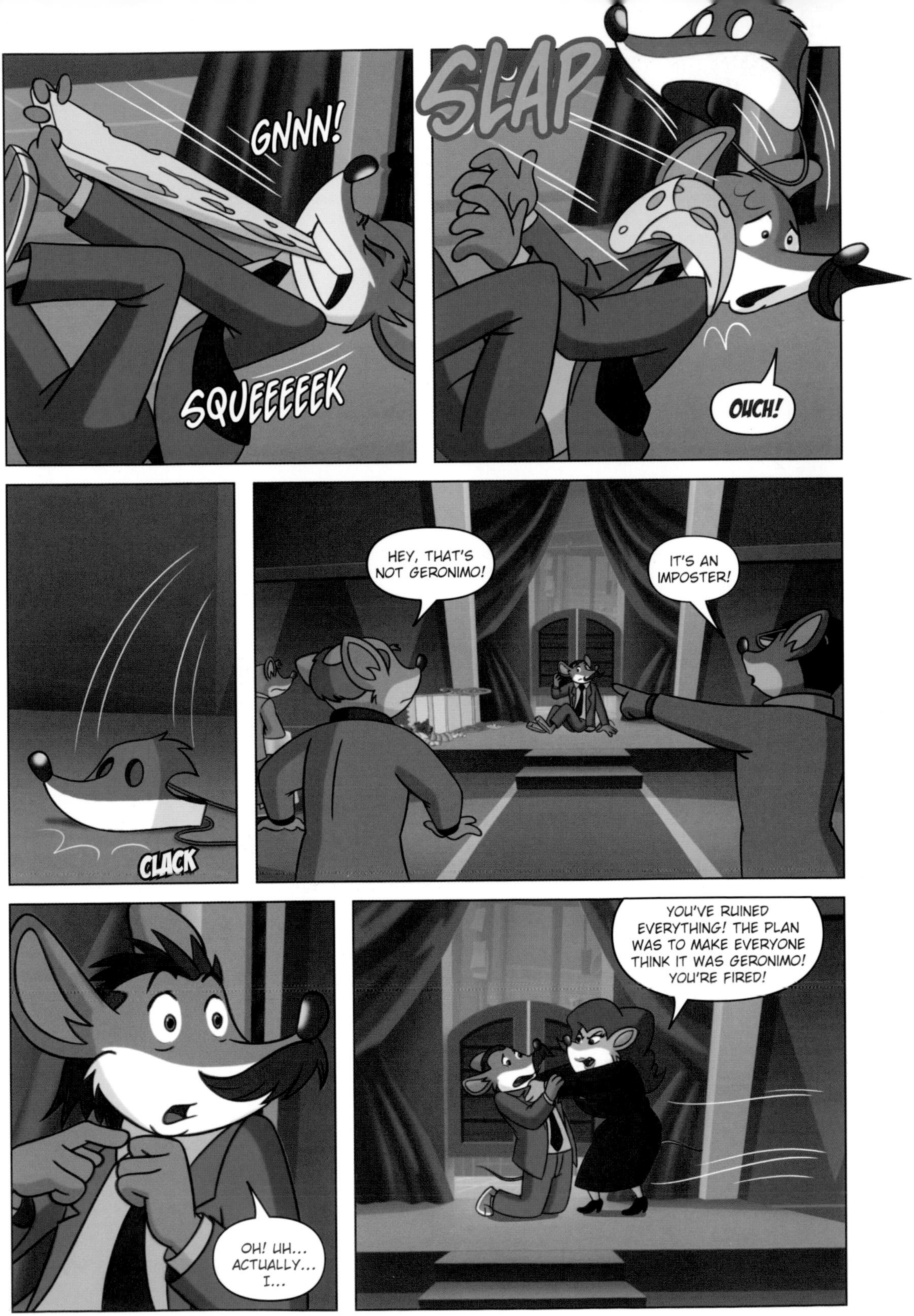
GNNN!
SQUEEEEEK
SLAP
OUCH!
CLACK
HEY, THAT'S NOT GERONIMO!
IT'S AN IMPOSTER!
OH! UH... ACTUALLY... I...
YOU'VE RUINED EVERYTHING! THE PLAN WAS TO MAKE EVERYONE THINK IT WAS GERONIMO! YOU'RE FIRED!

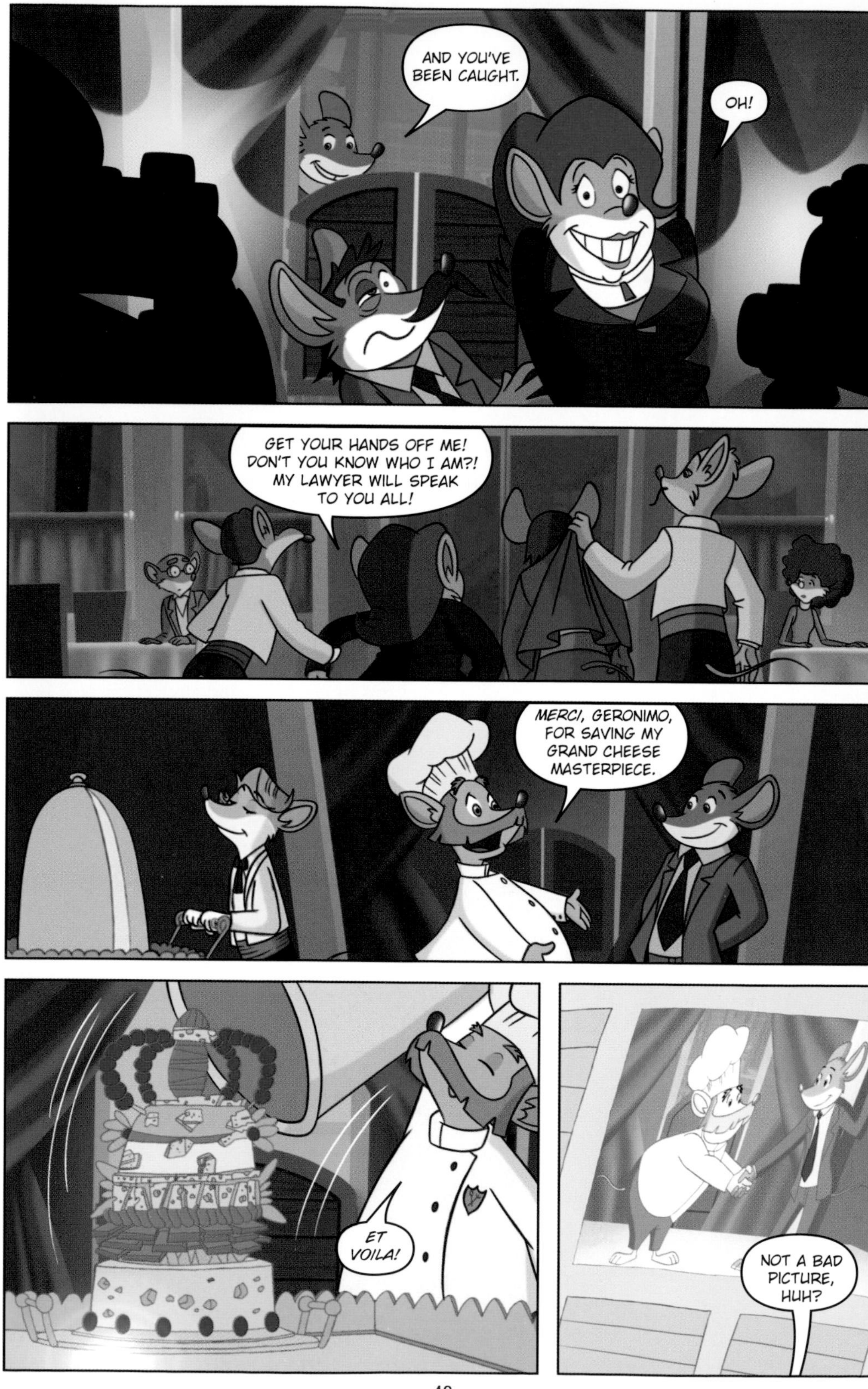
AND YOU'VE BEEN CAUGHT.
OH!
GET YOUR HANDS OFF ME! DON'T YOU KNOW WHO I AM?! MY LAWYER WILL SPEAK TO YOU ALL!
MERCI, GERONIMO, FOR SAVING MY GRAND CHEESE MASTERPIECE.
ET VOILA!
NOT A BAD PICTURE, HUH?

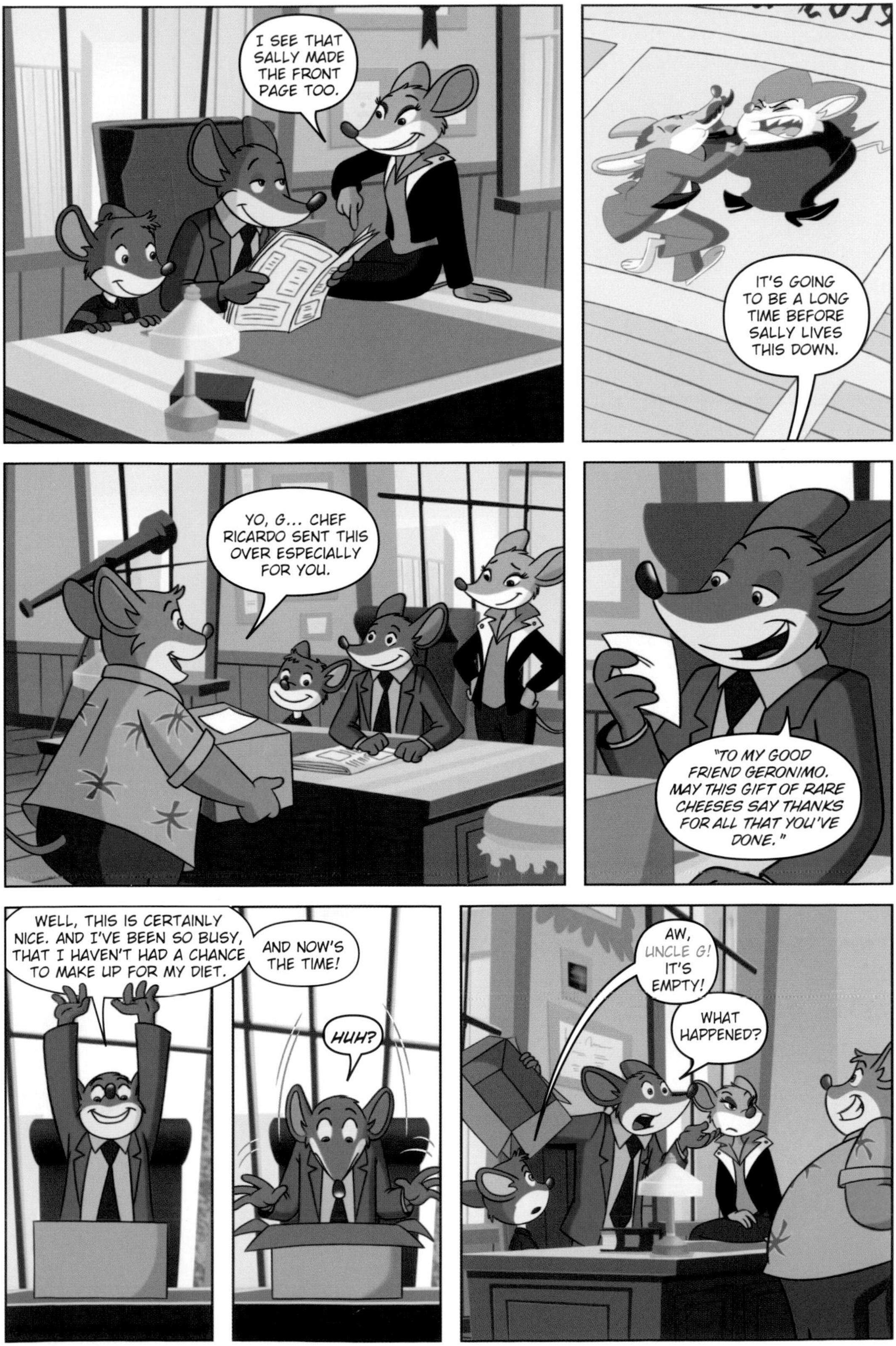
I SEE THAT SALLY MADE THE FRONT PAGE TOO.
IT'S GOING TO BE A LONG TIME BEFORE SALLY LIVES THIS DOWN.
YO, G... CHEF RICARDO SENT THIS OVER ESPECIALLY FOR YOU.
"TO MY GOOD FRIEND GERONIMO. MAY THIS GIFT OF RARE CHEESES SAY THANKS FOR ALL THAT YOU'VE DONE."
WELL, THIS IS CERTAINLY NICE. AND I'VE BEEN SO BUSY, THAT I HAVEN'T HAD A CHANCE TO MAKE UP FOR MY DIET.
AND NOW'S THE TIME!
HUH?
AW, UNCLE G! IT'S EMPTY!
WHAT HAPPENED?

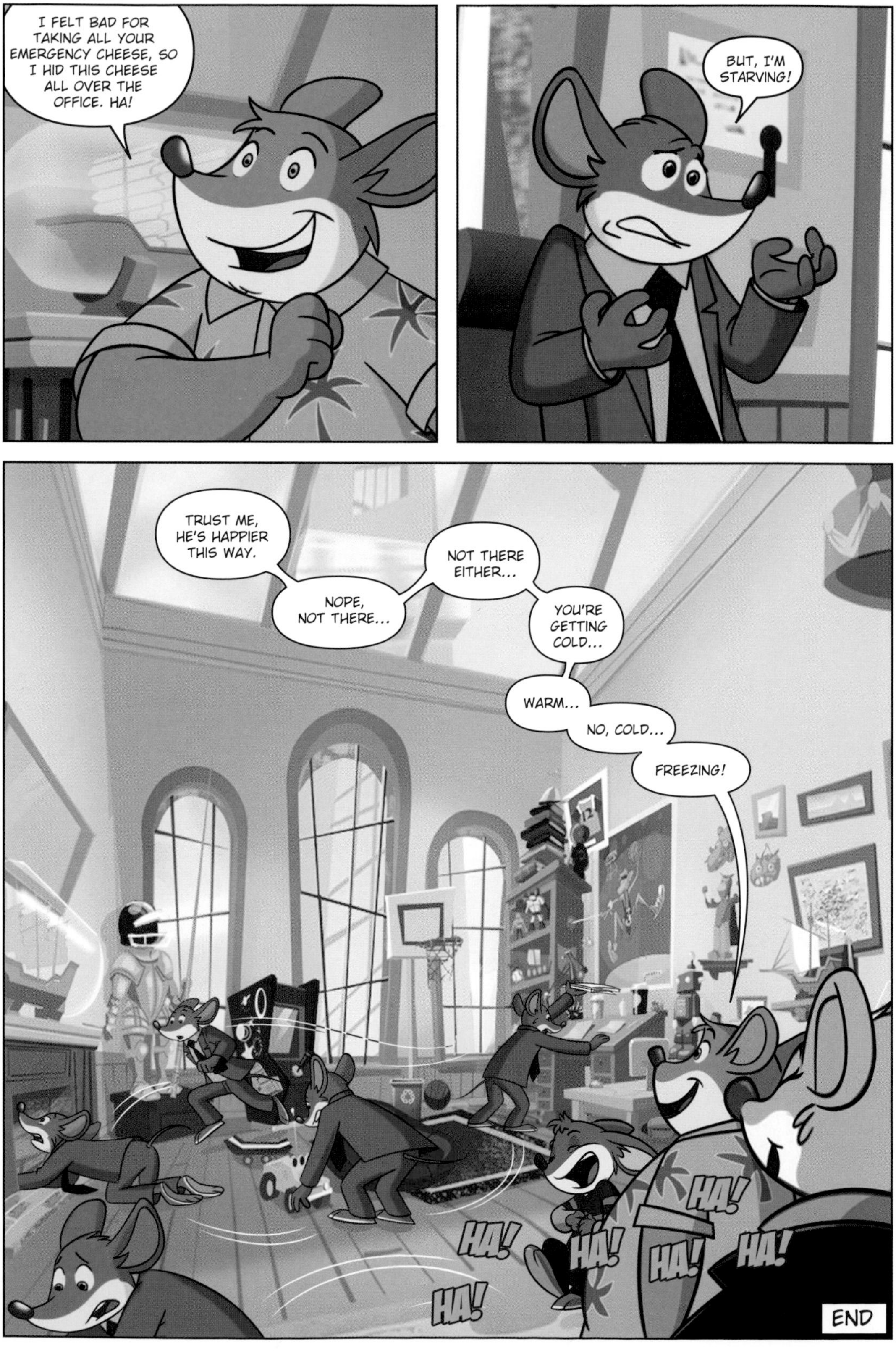
I FELT BAD FOR TAKING ALL YOUR EMERGENCY CHEESE, SO I HID THIS CHEESE ALL OVER THE OFFICE. HA!
BUT, I'M STARVING!
TRUST ME, HE'S HAPPIER THIS WAY.
NOPE, NOT THERE...
NOT THERE EITHER...
YOU'RE GETTING COLD...
WARM...
NO, COLD...
FREEZING!
HA!
HA!
HA!
HA!
HA!
END

Watch Out For PAPERCUTZ™

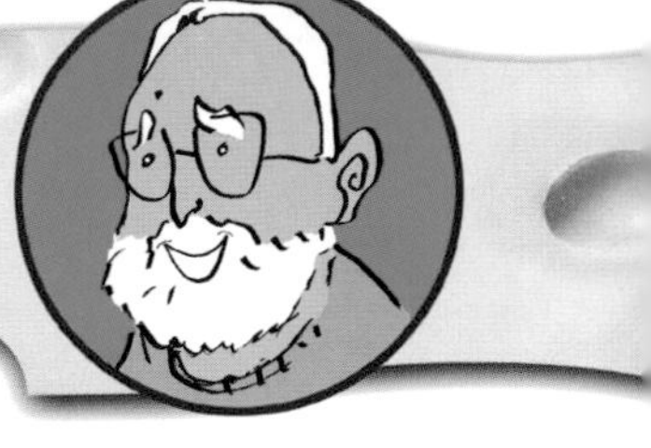

Welcome to the savory, succulent, and totally cheesy sixth GERONIMO STILTON REPORTER graphic novel, "Paws Off, Cheddarface!" the official comics adaptation of the sixth episode of Geronimo Stilton, Season One, written by Catherine Cuenca & Patrick Regnard, brought to you by Papercutz—those mousey-types dedicated to publishing great graphic novels for all ages. I'm Salicrup, ***Jim Salicrup,*** the Editor-in-Chief and Geronimo's Official Cheese-taster, here with more of *The Philosophy of Geronimo Stilton.* Essentially this philosophy is the guiding principles behind the creation of every Geronimo Stilton story, whether created for books, animation, or comics. You can check out the entire *Philosophy of Geronimo Stilton* online at geronimostilton.com. For this installment of *Watch Out for Papercutz*, we'll be taking a closer look at this part of the Philosophy…

GERONIMO STILTON AND FANTASY
The word "Fantasy" derives from the Greek work "phaino," meaning to show. It is the ability of the mind to invent stories or imaginary situations (without ties to reality, lived situations, or concrete references). It's fantasy that stimulates playing, to "make believe," in the sense of creating big, exciting adventures with your playmates. It must not be an escape from the real world, but a sort of trip from which you return having grown. Creative people see the world through different eyes and can see what other people can't. They are able to solve problems looking at them from another point of view using creativity, initiative, and optimism.

This may be a particularly tricky part of the philosophy to wrap your mind around, especially out of context (not being read along with the rest of the philosophy, that is). But there are several ways to interpret this particular point. First, involves the actual creation of Geronimo Stilton stories. While writers are encouraged to be as creative as possible, everyone still wants the adventures of Geronimo Stilton Reporter to be as believable as possible. So, while Geronimo and everyone else he encounters in his adventures may be talking, human-like mice (that's the fantasy part), everything else is treated fairly realistically (meaning everything else in the stories). For future writers out there, that's a valuable lesson to learn. That to make a fantastic idea more believable, set it in as realistic a world as possible. In other words, if every detail, every character, every action in a story is fantasy-based, the more unbelievable the story becomes (that's not to say you shouldn't try to write a story like that, just that it'll be more difficult to make it seem believable). Yet if there's only one fantasy element in a story, by making everything else in the story realistic, it helps the reader accept that that one fantasy element is possible.

Another way to interpret this aspect of Geronimo Stilton's philosophy, is understanding that creativity is not confined to creating art, such as stories, music, drawings, etc. Let me give you an example of exactly what I'm talking about. Over the years I've edited all kinds of comicbooks, and for quite awhile I edited a lot of super-hero comicbooks. As a result I became friends with many super-hero comic writers, and sometimes they'd tell me about a personal problem they had. I'd politely listen, and try to offer a helpful suggestion, but often I couldn't resist telling them that I found it a little funny that they make their living solving the problems of super heroes, and here they were stumped by an ordinary human problem. (Actually, that didn't always go over very well.) I'd suggest that very same creativity that would time after time save the super heroes, could probably solve their problems as well. And it usually did.

One of the greatest characters in literature is Sherlock Holmes, the great fictional detective created by Arthur Conan Doyle. Quite often Holmes would solve seemingly unsolvable mysteries by believing "once you eliminate the impossible, whatever remains, no matter how improbable, must be the truth." Geronimo Stilton often uses his creativity to figure out what's really going on, and by enjoying GERONIMO STILTON REPORTER, you may be training yourself to think more creatively. And you just thought you were enjoying a fun story!

Get ready for another fun story, coming your way in GERONIMO STILTON REPORTER #7 "Going Down to Chinatown." Check out the special preview starting on the next page… and then try to imagine what the rest of the story may be like. Then pick up GERONIMO STILTON REPORTER #7 "Going Down to Chinatown" and see how close you came to the real story!

Jim

STAY IN TOUCH!

EMAIL:	salicrup@papercutz.com
WEB:	papercutz.com
TWITTER:	@papercutzgn
INSTAGRAM:	@papercutzgn
FACEBOOK:	PAPERCUTZGRAPHICNOVELS
SNAIL MAIL:	Papercutz, 160 Broadway, Suite 700, East Wing, New York, NY 10038

Special Preview of GERONIMO STILTON REPORTER Graphic Novel #7
"Going Down to Chinatown!"

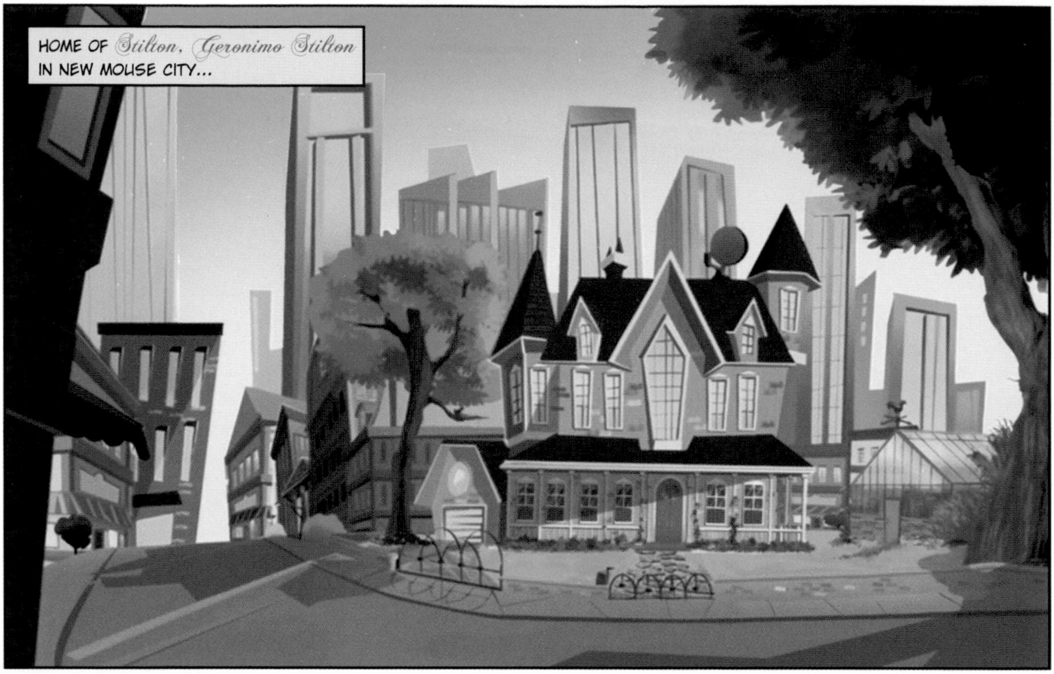
HOME OF Stilton, Geronimo Stilton
IN NEW MOUSE CITY...

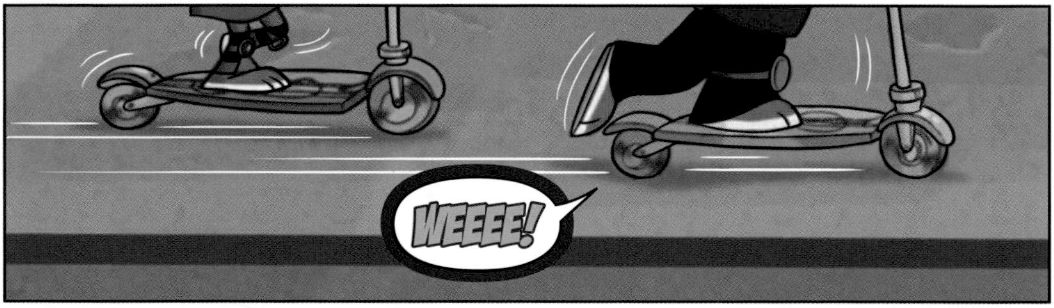
WEEEE!

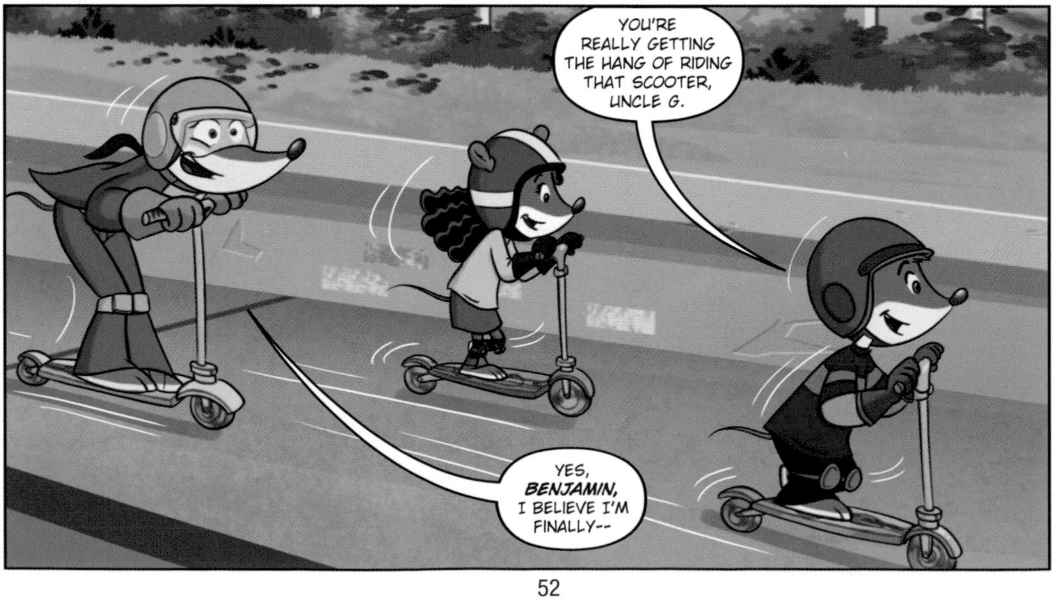
YOU'RE REALLY GETTING THE HANG OF RIDING THAT SCOOTER, UNCLE G.
YES, BENJAMIN, I BELIEVE I'M FINALLY--

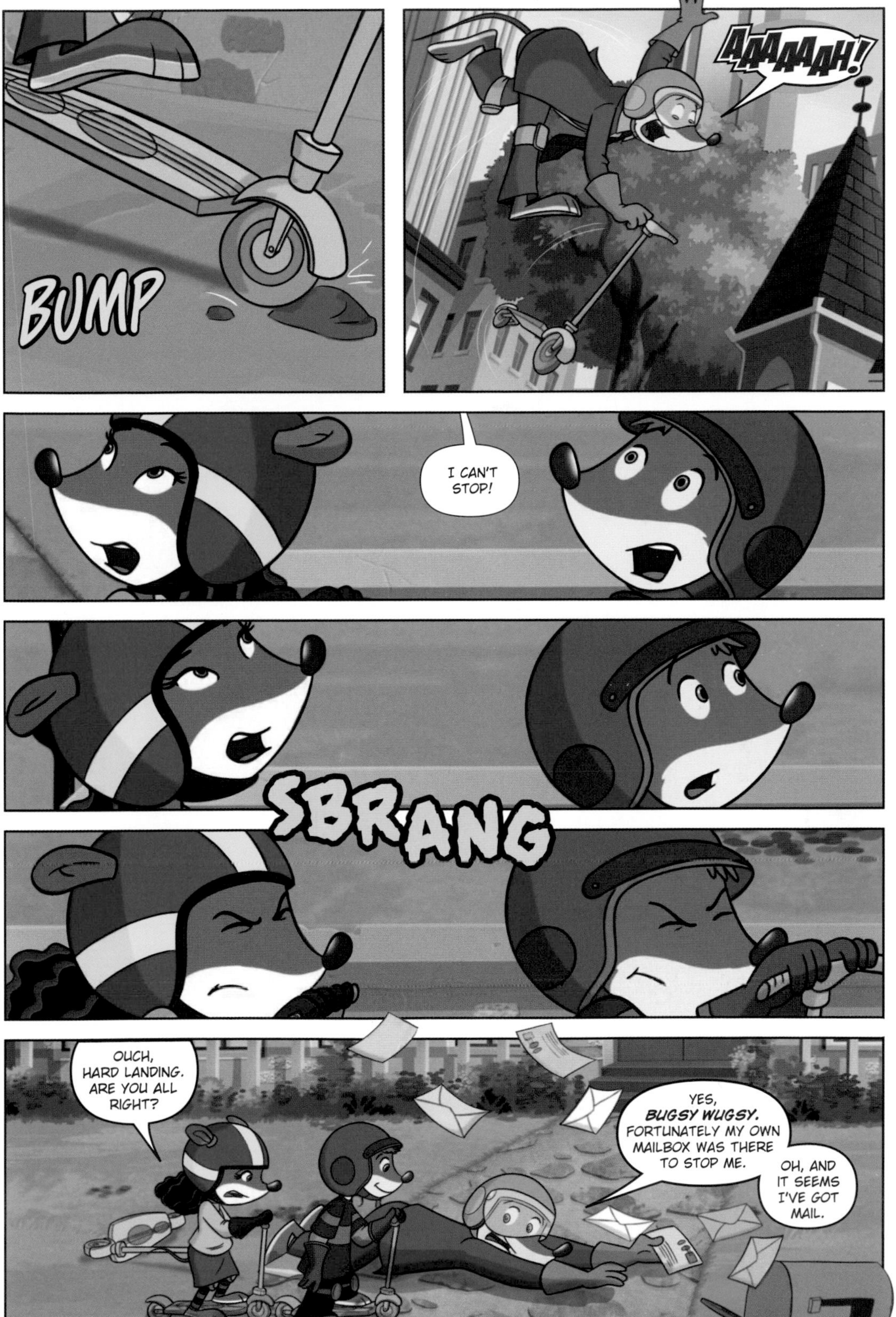
BUMP
AAAAAAH!
I CAN'T STOP!
SBRANG
OUCH, HARD LANDING. ARE YOU ALL RIGHT?
YES, **BUGSY WUGSY.** FORTUNATELY MY OWN MAILBOX WAS THERE TO STOP ME.
OH, AND IT SEEMS I'VE GOT MAIL.

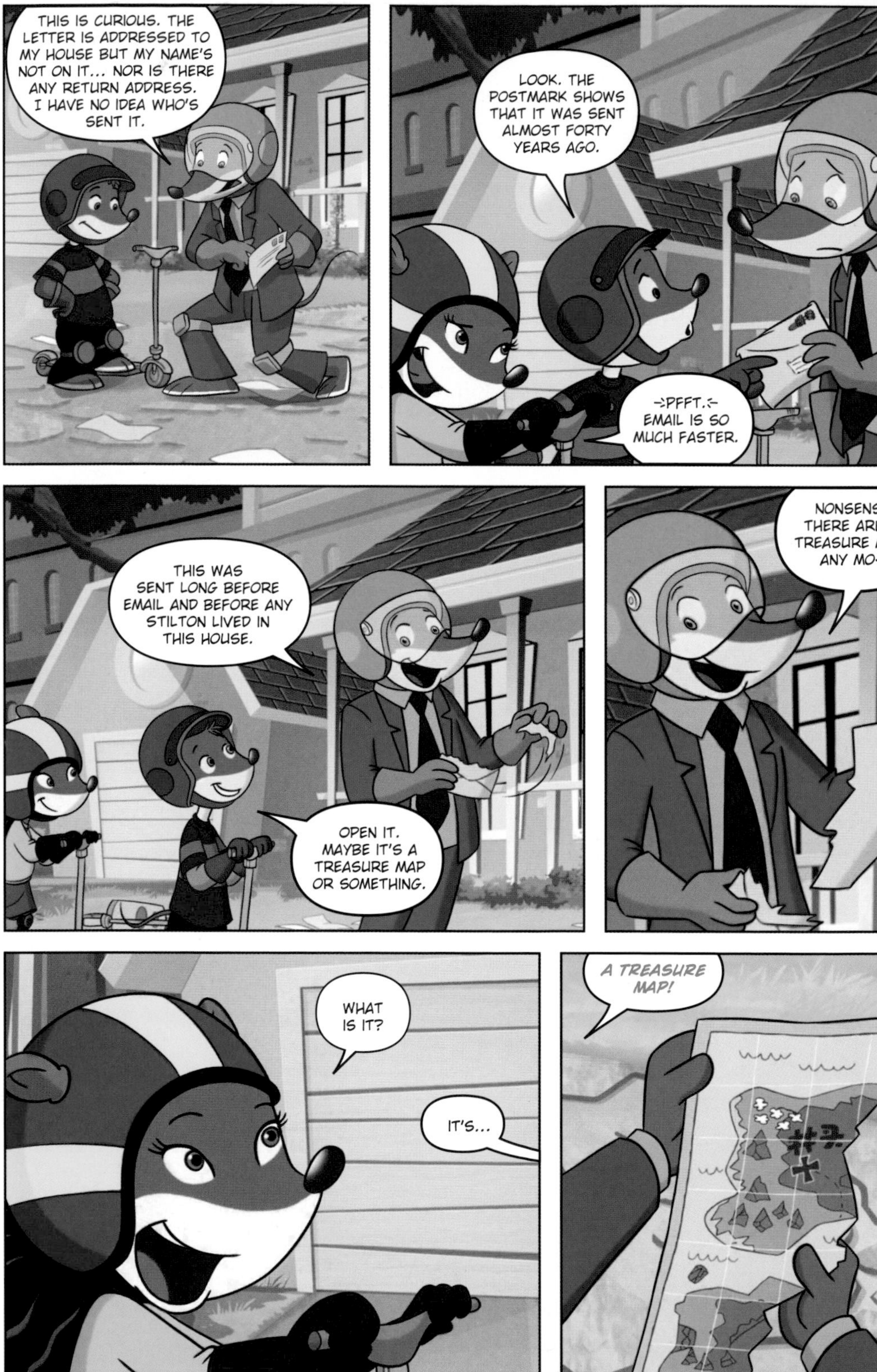
THIS IS CURIOUS. THE LETTER IS ADDRESSED TO MY HOUSE BUT MY NAME'S NOT ON IT... NOR IS THERE ANY RETURN ADDRESS. I HAVE NO IDEA WHO'S SENT IT.
LOOK. THE POSTMARK SHOWS THAT IT WAS SENT ALMOST FORTY YEARS AGO.
-PFFT.- EMAIL IS SO MUCH FASTER.
THIS WAS SENT LONG BEFORE EMAIL AND BEFORE ANY STILTON LIVED IN THIS HOUSE.
OPEN IT. MAYBE IT'S A TREASURE MAP OR SOMETHING.
NONSENSE, THERE AREN'T TREASURE MAPS ANY MO--
WHAT IS IT?
IT'S...
A TREASURE MAP!

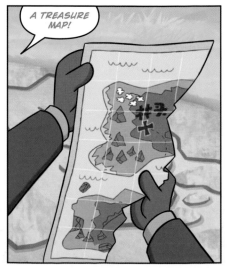

WELL, WHAT ARE WE WAITING FOR?

LET'S FOLLOW THAT MAP AND FIND US SOME TREASURE.

NOT SO FAST, *THEA*. REMEMBER, MY NAME WASN'T ON THE ENVELOPE THIS CAME IN, JUST MY ADDRESS. I DOUBT THIS MAP WAS EVEN MEANT FOR ME.

BESIDES, IT APPEARS WE ONLY HAVE ONE PIECE OF A LARGER MAP. SEE HERE WHERE THE EDGE IS TORN?

LOOK, THERE'RE LETTERS ON THE BACK.

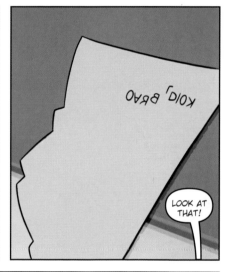

KOIQ, BRAVO

LOOK AT THAT!

"BLE-KREE-BLOOP..."?

OH, WELL, THAT MAKES NO SENSE.

TRAP!

OH, NO!

TINK

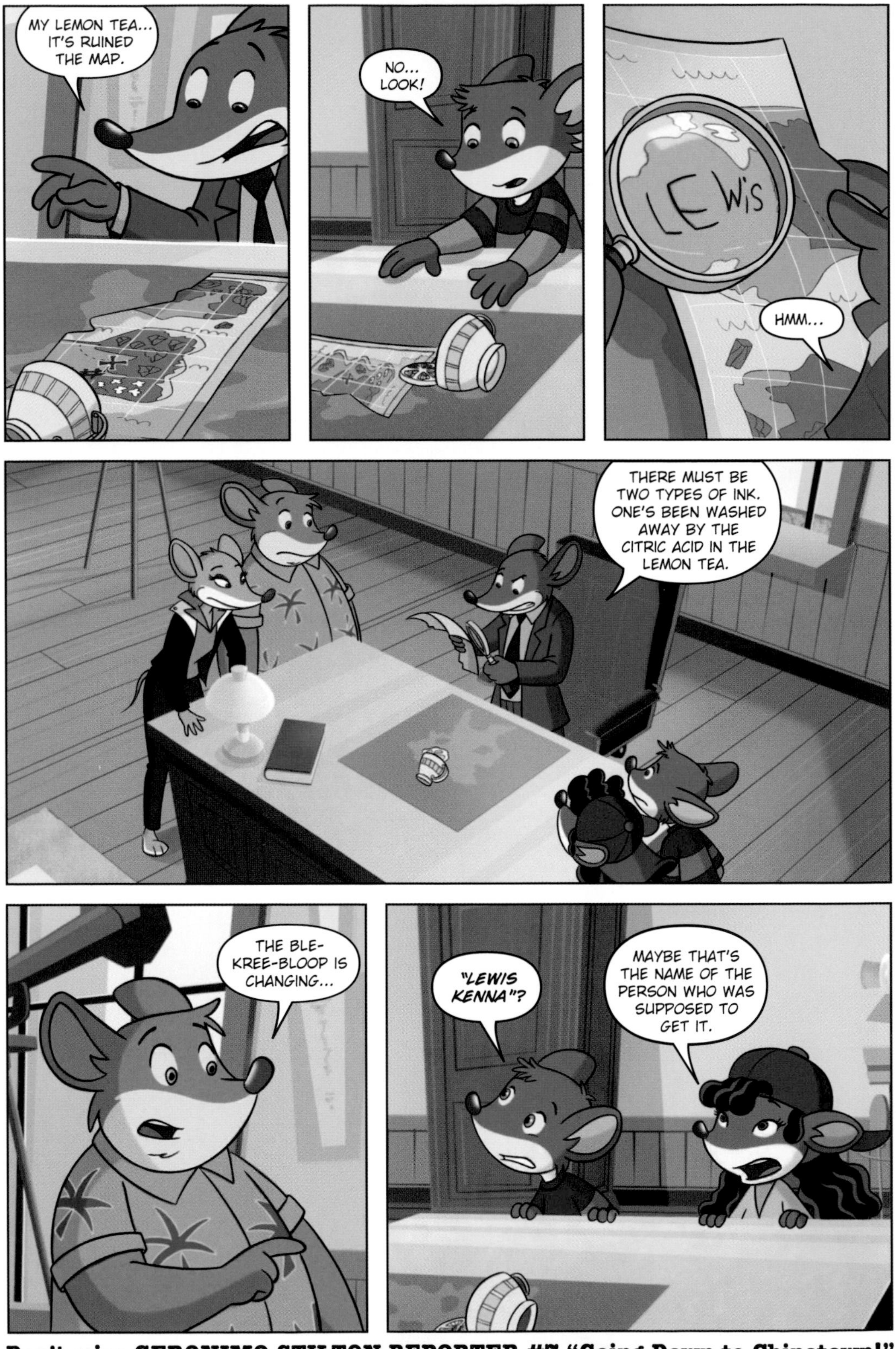
MY LEMON TEA... IT'S RUINED THE MAP.
NO... LOOK!
LEWIS
HMM...
THERE MUST BE TWO TYPES OF INK. ONE'S BEEN WASHED AWAY BY THE CITRIC ACID IN THE LEMON TEA.
THE BLE-KREE-BLOOP IS CHANGING...
"LEWIS KENNA"?
MAYBE THAT'S THE NAME OF THE PERSON WHO WAS SUPPOSED TO GET IT.

Don't miss GERONIMO STILTON REPORTER #7 "Going Down to Chinatown!" Coming soon!

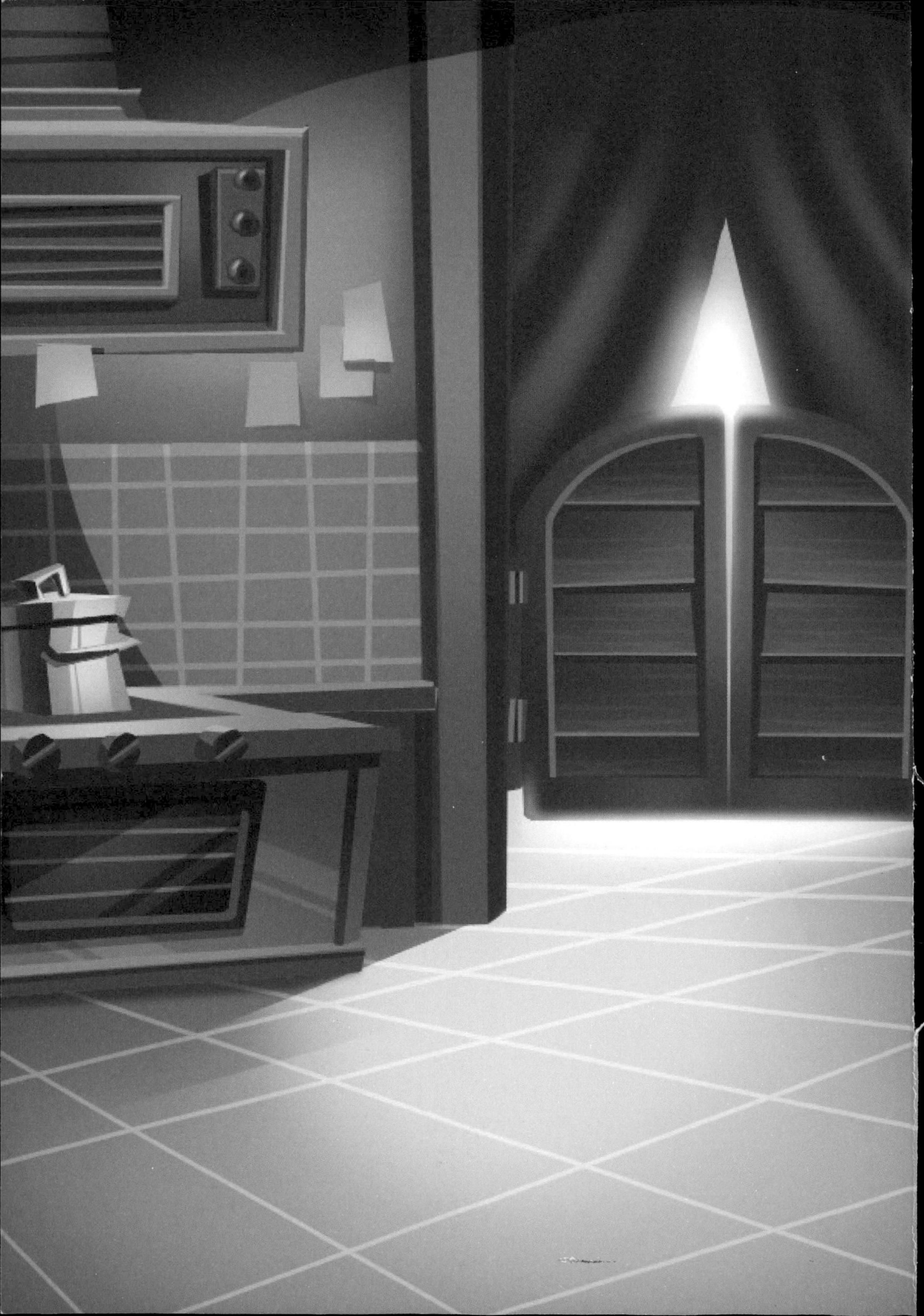